AND BABY MAKES THREE

"Luke, I've changed my mind. I'm not ready to be a mother."

Luke laughed. "Too late now—that horse is out of the barn. Now push a little harder, darlin'."

"You don't like how I'm doing it, you take over," Jessie snapped at him.

Minutes later, a sense of awe spread through him as he gazed at the precious baby in his arms. Luke desperately wished he could claim this child as his own. His and Jessie's.

But he knew that sooner or later Jessie would remember who he was and what he had done to ruin her life. The blame, no matter how hard she denied it, would be there between them.

But right now, for this one brief moment, they were united, a part of something incredibly special that he could hold in his heart the rest of his lonely days.

They had shared a miracle.

Dear Reader,

The holiday season is upon us—and we're in the midst of celebrating the arrival of our 1000th Special Edition! It is truly a season of cheer for all of us at Silhouette Special Edition.

We hope that you enjoy *The Pride of Jared MacKade* by *New York Times* bestselling author Nora Roberts. This is the second title of her bestselling THE MACKADE BROTHERS series, and the book is warm, wonderful—and not only Book 1000, but Nora's eightieth Silhouette novel! Thank you, Nora!

The celebration continues with the uplifting story of *Morgan's Rescue,* by Lindsay McKenna. This action-packed tale is the third installment of Lindsay's newest series, MORGAN'S MERCENARIES: LOVE AND DANGER. I know you won't want to miss a minute!

This month's HOLIDAY ELOPEMENTS title is a poignant, stirring story of the enduring power of love from Phyllis Halldorson—*The Bride and the Baby.*

Holidays are for children, and this month features many little ones with shining eyes and delighted laughter. In fact, we have a fun little element running through some of the books of unexpecting "dads" delivering babies! We hope you enjoy this unexpected bonus! Don't miss *Baby's First Christmas,* by Marie Ferrarella—the launch title of her marvelous cross-line series, THE BABY OF THE MONTH CLUB. Or Sherryl Woods's newest offering—*A Christmas Blessing*—the start of her Special Edition series, AND BABY MAKES THREE. Last, but not least, is the winsome *Mr. Angel* by Beth Henderson—a book full of warmth and cheer to warm wintry nights with love.

We hope that you enjoy this month of celebration. It's all due to you, our loyal readers. Happy holidays, and many thanks for your continued support from all of us at Silhouette Books!

Sincerely,

Tara Gavin
Senior Editor

Please address questions and book requests to:
Silhouette Reader Service
U.S.: 3010 Walden Ave., P.O. Box 1325, Buffalo, NY 14269
Canadian: P.O. Box 609, Fort Erie, Ont. L2A 5X3

SHERRYL WOODS
A CHRISTMAS BLESSING

Silhouette®

SPECIAL EDITION®

Published by Silhouette Books

America's Publisher of Contemporary Romance

For Kristi, my goddaughter, and Frankie, and their firstborn
son, Austin James—I wish you love and all the many
blessings of the season.

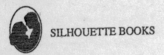 SILHOUETTE BOOKS

ISBN 0-373-24001-5

A CHRISTMAS BLESSING

Copyright © 1995 by Sherryl Woods

This edition published by arrangement with Harlequin Books S.A.

® and TM are trademarks of Harlequin Books S.A., used under
license. Trademarks indicated with ® are registered in the United States
Patent and Trademark Office, the Canadian Trade Marks Office and in
other countries.

Printed in U.S.A.

MOM-TO-BE STRANDED BY STORM

The first grandchild of rancher Harlan Adams was delivered by his son, Luke Adams, when sister-in-law and mother-to-be, Jessie Adams, was stranded by a blizzard. Angela Adams weighed 7 pounds 3 ounces.

Books by Sherryl Woods

SHERRYL WOODS

lives by the ocean, which, she says, provides daily inspiration for the romance in her soul. She further explains that her years as a television critic taught her about steamy plots and humor; her years as a travel editor took her to exotic locations; and her years as a crummy weekend tennis player taught her to stick with what she enjoyed most—writing. "What better way is there," Sherryl asks, "to combine all that experience than by creating romantic stories?" Sherryl loves to hear from her readers. You may write to her at P.O. Box 490326, Key Biscayne, FL 33149. A self-addressed, stamped envelope is appreciated for a reply.

Chapter One

Getting Consuela Martinez out of his kitchen was proving to be a much more difficult task than Luke Adams had ever envisioned. His housekeeper had found at least a dozen excuses for lingering, despite the fact that her brother was leaning on his car's horn and causing enough ruckus to deafen them all.

"Go, *amiga*," Luke pleaded. "Enjoy your holidays with your family. *Feliz Navidad!*"

Consuela ignored the instructions and the good wishes. "The freezer is filled with food," she reminded him, opening the door to show him for the fourth time. Though there were literally dozens of precooked, neatly labeled packages, a worried frown puckered her brow. "It will be enough?"

"More than enough," he assured her.

"But not if you have guests," she concluded, removing her coat. "I should stay. The holidays are no time for a good housekeeper to be away."

"I won't be having any guests," Luke said tightly, picking the coat right back up and practically forcing her into it. "And if I do, I am perfectly capable of whipping up a batch of chips and dip."

"Chips and dip," she muttered derisively.

She added a string of Spanish Luke felt disinclined to translate. He caught the general drift; it wasn't complimentary. After all this time, though, Consuela should know that he wasn't the type to host a lot of extravagant, foolish parties. Leave that sort of thing to his brother Jordan or his parents. His brother thrived on kissing up to his business associates and his parents seemed to think that filling the house with strangers meant they were well loved and well respected.

"Consuela, go!" he ordered, barely curbing his impatience. "*Vaya con Dios*. I'll be fine. I am thirty-two years old. I've been out of my playpen for a long time."

One of the dangers of hiring an ex-nanny as a housekeeper, he'd discovered, was the tendency she had to forget that her prior charge had grown up. Yet he could no more have fired Consuela than he could have his own mother. In truth, for all of her hovering and bossiness, she was the single most important constant in his life. Which was a pretty pitiful comment on the state of his family, he decided ruefully.

Consuela's unflinching, brown-eyed gaze pinned him. Hands on ample hips, she squared off against him. "You will go to your parents' on Christmas, *sí?* The holidays are a time for families to be together. You have stayed away too long."

"Yes," he lied. He had no intention of going anywhere, especially not to his parents' house where everyone would be mourning, not celebrating, thanks to him.

"They will have enough help for all of the parties that are planned?"

Luke bit back a groan. "Consuela, you know perfectly well they will," he said patiently. "The place is crawling with your very own nieces and nephews. My parents haven't had to cook, clean or sneeze without assistance since you took over the running of that household forty years ago before they'd even met. When you came over here to work for me, you handpicked your cousin to replace you. Maritza is very good, yes?"

"*Sí,*" she conceded.

"This trip to see your family in Mexico is my present to you. It's long overdue. You said yourself not sixty seconds ago that the holidays are meant for families. You have not seen your own for several years. Your mother is almost ninety. You cry every time a letter comes from her."

"After all these years, I get homesick, that's true. I am a very emotional person, not like some people," she said pointedly.

Luke ignored the jibe. "Well, this is your chance to see for yourself how your mother is doing. Now stop dawdling and go before you miss your plane and before your brother busts our eardrums with that horn of his.''

Consuela still appeared torn between duty to him and a longing to see her mother. Finally she heaved a sigh of resignation and buttoned her coat. "I will go," she said grudgingly. "But I will worry the whole time. You are alone too much, *niño.*"

It had been a long time since anyone had thought of Luke Adams as a little boy. Unfortunately, Consuela would probably never get the image out of her head, despite the fact that he was over six feet tall, operated a thriving ranch and had built himself a house twice the size of the very lavish one he'd grown up in.

"Ever since—" she began.

"Enough," Luke said in a low, warning tone that silenced her more quickly than any shout would have.

Tears of sympathy sprang to her eyes, and she wrapped her plump arms around him in a fierce hug that had Luke wincing. For a sixty-year-old woman she was astonishingly strong. He didn't want her weeping for him, though. He didn't want her pity. And he most definitely didn't want her dredging up memories of Erik, the brother who'd died barely seven months ago, the brother whose death he'd caused.

"Go," he said more gently. "I will see you in the new year."

She reached up and patted his cheek, a gesture she dared only rarely. *"Te amo, niño."*

Luke's harsh demeanor softened at once. "I love you, too, Consuela."

The truth of it was that she was about the only human being on the face of the earth to whom he could say that without reservation. Even before Erik's death had split the family apart, Luke had had his share of difficulties with his father's attempted ironclad grip on his sons. His mother had always been too much in love with her husband to bother much with the four boys she had borne him. And Luke had battled regularly with his younger brothers, each of them more rebellious than the other. Erik had been a year younger, only thirty-one when he'd died. Jordan was thirty, Cody twenty-seven. Consuela had been the steadying influence on all of them, adults and children.

"Te amo, mi amiga," Luke said, returning her fierce hug.

Consuela was still calling instructions as she crossed the porch and climbed into her brother's car. For all he knew she was still shouting them as the car sped off down the lane to the highway, kicking up a trail of dust in its wake.

Alone at last, he thought with relief when Consuela was finally gone from view. Blessed silence for two whole weeks. His cattle were pastured on land far from the main house and were being tended by his foreman and a crew of volunteers from among the hands. The ranch's business affairs were tied up through the beginning of the new year. He had no obligations at all.

He opened a cupboard, withdrew an unopened bottle of Jack Daniel's whiskey from the supply he'd ordered, ostensibly to take along as gifts to all the holiday parties to which he'd been invited. He pulled down a nice, tall glass, filled it with ice and headed for his den and the big leather chair behind his desk.

Uncapping the bottle, he poured a shot, doubled it, then shrugged and filled the glass to the rim. No point in pretending he didn't intend to get blind, stinking drunk. No point in pretending he didn't intend to stay that way until the whole damned holiday season had passed by in a blur.

Just as he lifted the glass to his lips, he caught sight of the wedding photo on the corner of his desk, the one he'd turned away so that he wouldn't have to see Erik's smile or the radiance on Erik's wife's face. He'd destroyed two lives that day, three if he counted his own worthless existence. Erik was dead and buried, but Jessie's life had been devastated as surely as if she had been in that accident with him.

A familiar knot formed in his stomach, a familiar pain encircled his heart. He lifted his glass in a mockery of a toast. "To you, little brother."

The unaccustomed liquor burned going down, but in the space of a heartbeat it sent a warm glow shimmering through him. If one sip was good, two were better, and the whole damned bottle promised oblivion.

He drank greedily, waiting to forget, waiting for relief from the unceasing anguish, from the unending guilt.

The phone rang, stopped, then rang again. The old grandfather clock in the hall chimed out each passing hour as dusk fell, then darkness.

But even sitting there all alone in the dark with a belly full of the best whiskey money could buy, Luke couldn't shut off the memories. With a curse, he threw the bottle across the room, listened with satisfaction as it shattered against the cold, stone fireplace.

Finally, worn out, he fell into a troubled sleep. It wasn't his brother's face he saw as he passed out, though. It was Jessie's—the woman who should have been his.

The sky was dark as pitch and the roads were icing over. Jessie Adams squinted through the car's foggy windshield and wondered why she'd ever had the bright idea of driving clear across Texas for the holidays, instead of letting her father-in-law send his pilot for her. She wasn't even sure how Harlan and Mary Adams had persuaded her that she still belonged with them now that Erik was gone.

She'd always felt like an outsider in that big white Colonial house that looked totally incongruous sitting in the middle of a sprawling West Texas ranch. Someone in the family, long before Harlan's time, had fled the South during the Civil War. According to the oft-told legend, the minute they'd accumulated enough cash, they'd built an exact replica of the mansion they'd left behind in ashes. And like the old home, they'd called it White Pines, though she couldn't recall ever seeing a single pine within a thirty-mile radius.

The bottom line was the Adamses were rich as could be and had ancestry they could trace back to the *Mayflower*, while Jessie didn't even know who her real parents had been. Her adoptive parents had sworn they didn't know and had seemed so hurt by her wanting to find out that she'd reluctantly dropped any notion of searching for answers.

By the time they'd died, she'd pushed her need to know aside. She had met Erik, by then. Marrying him and adjusting to his large, boisterous family had been more than enough to handle. Mary Adams was sweet as could be, if a little superior at times, but Erik's father and his three brothers were overwhelming. Harlan Adams was a stern and domineering parent, sure of himself about everything. He was very much aware of himself as head of what he considered to be a powerful dynasty. As for Erik's brothers, she'd never met a friendlier, more flirtatious crew, and she had worked in her share of bars to make ends meet while she'd been in college.

Except for Luke. The oldest, he was a brooder. Dark and silent, Luke had been capable of tremendous kindness, but rarely did he laugh and tease as his brothers did. The expression in the depths of his eyes was bleak, as if he was bearing in silence some terrible hurt deep in his soul. There had been odd moments when she'd felt drawn to him, when she'd felt she understood better than anyone his seeming loneliness in the midst of a family gathering, when she had longed to put a smile on his rugged, handsome face.

That compelling sense of an unspoken connection had been ripped to shreds on the day Luke had come to tell her that her husband was in the hospital and unlikely to make it. In a short burst riddled with agonized guilt, he'd added that he was responsible for the overturning of the tractor that had injured Erik. He'd made no apologies, offered no excuses. He'd simply stated the facts, seen to it that she got to the hospital, made sure the rest of the family was there to support her, then walked away. He'd avoided her from that moment on. Avoided everyone in the family ever since, from what Harlan and Mary had told her. He seemed to be intent on punishing himself, they complained sadly.

If Luke hadn't been steering clear of White Pines, Jessie wasn't at all sure she would have been able to accept the invitation to come for the holidays. Seeing Luke's torment, knowing it mirrored her own terrible mix of grief and guilt was simply too painful. She hated him for costing her the one person to whom she'd really mattered.

Searching for serenity, she had fled the ranch a month after Erik's death, settled in a new place on the opposite side of the state, gotten a boring job that paid the bills and prepared to await the birth of her child. Erik's baby. Her only link to the husband she had adored, but hadn't always understood.

She stopped the dark thoughts before they could spoil her festive holiday mood. There was no point at all in looking back. She had her future—she rested a hand on her stomach—and she had her baby, though goodness knows she hadn't planned on being a single parent. Sometimes the prospect terrified her.

She found a station playing Christmas carols, turned up the volume and sang along, as she began the last hundred and fifty miles or so of the once familiar journey back to White Pines. Her back was aching like the dickens and she'd forgotten how difficult driving could be when her protruding belly forced her to put the seat back just far enough to make reaching the gas and brake pedals a strain.

"No problem," she told herself sternly. A hundred miles or more in this part of the world was nothing. She had snow tires on, a terrific heater, blankets in the trunk for an emergency and a batch of homemade fruitcakes in the back that would keep her from starving if she happened to get stranded.

The persistent ache in her back turned into a more emphatic pain that had her gasping.

"What the dickens?" she muttered as she hit the brake, slowed and paused to take a few deep breaths. Fortunately there was little traffic to worry about on the unexpectedly bitter cold night. She stayed on the side of the road for a full five minutes to make sure there wouldn't be another spasm on the heels of the first.

Satisfied that it had been nothing more than a pinched nerve or a strained muscle, she put the car back in gear and drove on.

It was fifteen minutes before the next pain hit, but it was a doozy. It brought tears to her eyes. Again, pulling to the side of the road, she scowled down at her belly.

"This is not the time," she informed the impertinent baby. "You will not be born in a car in the middle of nowhere with no doctor in sight, do you understand me? That's the deal, so get used to it and settle down. You're not due for weeks yet. Four weeks to be exact, so let's have no more of these pains, okay?"

Apparently the lecture worked. Jessie didn't feel so much as a twinge for another twenty miles. She was about to congratulate herself on skirting disaster, when a contraction gripped her so fiercely she thought she'd lose control of the car.

"Oh, sweet heaven," she muttered in a tone that was part prayer, part curse. There was little doubt in her mind now that she was going into labor. Denying it seemed pointless, to say nothing of dangerous. She had to take a minute here and think of a plan.

On the side of the road again, she turned on the car's overhead light, took out her map and searched for some sign of a hospital. If there was one within fifty miles, she couldn't spot it. She hadn't passed a house for miles, either, and she was still far from Harlan and Mary's, probably a hundred miles at least. She could make that in a couple of hours or less, if the roads were clear, but they weren't. She was driving at a safe crawl. It could take her hours to get to White Pines at that pace.

There was someplace she could go that would be closer, someplace only five miles or so ahead, unless she'd lost her bearings. It was the last place on earth she'd ever intended to wind up, the very last place she would want her baby to be born: Luke's ranch.

Consuela would be there, she consoled herself as she resigned herself to dropping by unannounced to deliver a baby. Luke probably didn't want to see her any more than she wanted to see him. And what man wanted any part of a woman's labor, unless she happened to be his wife? Luke probably wouldn't be able to turn her over to Consuela fast enough. With all those vacant rooms, they probably wouldn't even bump into each other in the halls.

Jessie couldn't see that she had any choice. The snow had turned to blizzard conditions. The world around her was turning into a snow-covered wonderland, as dangerous as it was beautiful. The tires were beginning to skid and spin on the road. The contractions were maybe ten minutes apart. She'd be lucky to make it these few miles to Luke's. Forget going any farther.

The decision made with gut-deep reluctance, she accomplished the drive by sheer force of will. When she finally spotted the carved gate announcing the ranch, she skidded to a halt and wept with relief. She still had a mile of frozen, rutted lane to the house, but that would be a breeze compared to the five she'd just traveled.

A hard contraction, the worst yet, gripped her and had her screaming out loud. She clung to the steering wheel, panting as she'd seen on TV, until it passed. Sweat streamed down her face.

"Come on, sweet thing," she pleaded with the baby. "Only a few more minutes. Don't you dare show up until I get to the house."

She couldn't help wondering when that would be. There was no beckoning light in the distance, no looming shape of the house. Surely, though, it couldn't be much farther.

She drove on, making progress by inches, it seemed. At last she spotted the house, dark as coal against the blinding whiteness around it. Not a light on anywhere. No bright holiday decorations blinking tiny splashes of color onto the snow.

"Luke Adams, you had better be home," she muttered as she hauled herself out from behind the wheel at last.

Standing on shaky legs, she began the endless trek through the deepening snow, cursing and clutching her stomach as she bent over with yet another ragged pain. The wind-whipped snow stung her cheeks and mingled with tears. The already deepening drifts made walking treacherous and slow.

"A little farther," she encouraged herself. Three steps. Four. One foot onto the wide sweep of a porch. Then the other. She had made it! She paused and sucked in a deep breath, then looked around her.

The desolate air about the place had only intensified as she'd drawn closer. There was no wreath of evergreens on the front door, no welcoming light shining on the porch or from any of the rooms that she could detect. For the first time, she allowed a panicky thought. What if she had made it this far, only to find herself still alone? What if Luke had packed his bags and flown away for the holidays?

"Please, God, let someone be here," she prayed as she hit the doorbell again and again, listening to the chime echo through the house. She pounded on the glass, shouted, then punched the doorbell again.

She heard a distant crash, a loud oath, then another crash. Apparently Luke was home, she thought dryly, as she began another insistent round of doorbell ringing.

"For cripe's sakes, hold your horses, dammit!"

A light switch was thrown and the porch was illuminated in a warm yellow glow. Finally, just as another contraction ripped through Jessie, the door was flung open.

She was briefly aware of the thunderstruck expression on Luke's face and his disheveled state, only marginally aware of the overpowering scent of alcohol.

And then, after a murmured greeting she doubted made a lick of sense, she collapsed into the arms of the man who'd killed her husband.

Chapter Two

"What in blazes...?"

Luke folded his arms around the bundled-up form who'd just pitched forward. Blinking hard in an attempt to get his eyes to focus, he zeroed in on a face that had once been burned into his brain, a face he'd cursed himself for cherishing when he had no right at all. He'd seen that precious face only minutes ago in the sweetest dream he'd ever had. For an instant he wondered if he was still dreaming.

No, he could feel her shape, crushed against his chest. He drank in the sight of her. Her long, black hair was tucked up in a stocking cap. Her cheeks, normally pale as cream, had been tinted a too-bright pink by the cold. Her blue eyes were shadowed with what might have been pain, but there was no mistaking his sister-in-law.

"Jessie," he whispered, worriedly taking in the lines of strain on her forehead, the trickle of sweat that was likely to turn to ice if he didn't get her out of the freezing night in a hurry.

When in hell had it turned so bitter? he wondered, shivering himself. There hadn't been a snowflake in sight when he'd sent Consuela off. Now he couldn't see a patch of uncovered ground anywhere. Couldn't see much of anything beyond the porch, for that matter.

More important than any of that, what was his sister-in-law doing here of all places? Was she ill? Feverish? She would have had to be practically delusional or desperate to turn up on his doorstep.

He scooped her up, rocking back on his heels with the unexpected weight of her, startled that the little slip of a thing he'd remembered was bulging out of her coat. She moaned and clutched at her belly, shuddering against him.

She's going to have a baby, he realized at last, finally catching on to what would have been obvious to anyone who was not in an alcohol-altered state of mind. No one in the family had told him that. Not that he'd done more than exchange pleasantries with any of them in months. And Jessie would have been the last person they would have mentioned. Everyone walked on eggshells around him when it came to anything having to do with his late brother. If only they had known, if only they had realized that his guilt was compounded because he'd fallen for Erik's wife, they would never have spoken to him at all.

"You're going to have a baby," he announced in an awestruck tone.

Bright blue eyes, dulled by pain, snapped open. "You always were quick, Lucas," Jessie said tartly. "Do you suppose you could get me to a bed and find Consuela before I deliver right here in the foyer?"

"You're going to have a baby *now?*" he demanded incredulously, as the immediacy of the problem sank in. He would have dropped her if she hadn't been clinging to his neck with the grip of a championship arm wrestler.

"That would be my best guess," she agreed.

Luke was so stunned—so damned drunk—he couldn't seem to come to any rational decision. If Jessie had realized his condition, she would have headed for the barn and relied on one of the horses for help. He had a mare who was probably more adept at deliveries than he was at this precise moment. His old goat, Chester, was pretty savvy, too. Jessie would have been in better hands with them, than she likely was with him.

"Lucas?" Her voice was low and sweet as honey. "Could you please..."

He sighed just listening to her. The sweetest little voice in all of Texas.

"Get me into a bed!"

The shout accomplished what nothing else had. He began to move. He staggered ever so slightly, but he got her into the closest bedroom, his, and settled her in the middle of sheets still rumpled from the previous night. And several nights before that, as near as he could recall. He'd ordered Consuela to stay the hell out of his bedroom after he'd found little packets of some sweet-smelling stuff in his sock drawer.

He stood gazing down at Jessie, rhapsodizing to himself about her presence in his bed, marveling at the size of that belly, awestruck by the fact that she was going to have a baby here and now.

"Luke," she said in a raspy voice that was edged with tension. "I'm going to need a little help here."

"Help?" he repeated blankly.

"My clothes."

"Oh." He blinked rapidly as he watched her trying to struggle out of her coat. Awkwardly, she shrugged it off one shoulder, then the other. When she started to fumble with the buttons on her blouse, his throat worked and his pulse zoomed into the stratosphere.

"Lucas!"

The shout got his attention. "Oh, yeah. Right," he said and tried to help with the buttons.

For a man who'd undressed any number of women in his time, he was suddenly all thumbs. In fact, getting Jessie out of her clothes—the simple cotton blouse, the oddly made jeans, the lacy bra and panties—was an act of torture no man should have to endure. Trying to be helpful, she wriggled and squirmed in a way that brought his fingers into contact with warm, smooth skin far too frequently. Trying to look everywhere except at her wasn't helping him with the task either. Every glimpse of bare flesh made his knees go weak.

The second she was stripped bare, he muffled a groan, averted his gaze and hunted down one of his shirts. He did it for his own salvation, not because she seemed aware of anything except the demands her baby was making on her body. Surely there was a special place in hell for a man whose thoughts were on sex when a woman was about to have a baby right before his eyes.

She looked tiny—except for that impressively swollen belly—and frightened as a doe caught in a hunter's sights. He felt a powerful need to comfort her, if only he could string an entire sentence together without giving away his inebriated state. If she knew precisely how drunk he was, she wouldn't be scared. She'd be flat-out terrified, and rightfully so. He wasn't so serene himself.

"Where's Consuela?" she asked, then let out a scream that shook the rafters. She latched on to his hand so hard he was sure that at least three bones cracked. That grip did serve a purpose, though. It snapped him back to reality. Pain had a way of making a man focus on the essentials.

The baby clearly wasn't going to wait for him to sober up. It wasn't going to wait for a doctor, even if one could make it to the ranch on the icy roads, which Luke doubted.

"Consuela's in Mexico by now," he confessed without thinking. "She left earlier today." When panic immediately darkened her eyes, he instinctively patted her hand. "It's going to be okay, darlin'. Don't you worry about a thing."

"I'm... not... worried," she said between gasps. "Shouldn't you boil water or something?"

Water? Water was good, he decided. He had no idea what he'd do with it, but if it got him out of this bedroom for five seconds so he could try to gather his scattered thoughts, it had to be good. Coffee would be even better. Gallons of it.

"You'll be okay for a minute?" He grabbed a key chain made of braided leather off his dresser and gave it to her. "Hang on to this if another pain hits while I'm gone, okay? Bite into it or something." It had worked for cowboys being operated on under primitive conditions, or so he'd read. Of course, they'd also been liberally dosed with alcohol at the time.

Jessie's blue eyes regarded the leather doubtfully, but she nodded gamely. "Hurry, Luke. I don't know much about labor, but I don't think there's a lot of time left."

"I'll be back before you know it," he promised. Stone-cold sober, if he could manage it.

He fumbled the first pot he grabbed, spilled water everywhere, then finally got it onto the stove with the gas flame turned to high. With a couple of false starts, he got the coffee going as well, strong enough to wake the dead, which was pretty much how he felt.

For a moment he clung to the counter and tried to steady himself. It was going to be okay, he vowed. He'd delivered foals and calves. How much different could delivering a baby be? Of course, mares and cows had a pretty good notion of what they were doing. They didn't need a lot of assistance from him unless they got into trouble.

Jessie, on the other hand, seemed even more be-mused by this state of affairs than he was. She'd ob-viously been counting on a doctor, a team of comforting nurses, a nice, sterile delivery room and plenty of high-tech equipment. A shot of some kind of painkiller, too, more than likely. What she was get-ting was a drunken amateur in an isolated ranch house. It hardly seemed fair after all she'd already been through. After all he'd put her through, he amended.

An agonized scream cut through the air and sent panic slicing through him. He tore down the hall to the bedroom. He found her panting, her face scrunched up with pain, sweat beading up on her brow and pouring down her cheeks. Damned if he didn't think she looked beautiful, anyway. The door to that place in hell gaped wider.

"You okay?" he asked, then shook himself. "Sorry. Dumb question. Of course, you're not okay."

He grabbed a clean washcloth from the linen closet, dashed into the bathroom to soak it with cool water, then wiped her brow. He might not be exactly sober yet, but his brain was beginning to function and his limbs were following orders. For the first time, he honestly believed they could get through this without calamity striking.

"You're doing fine," he soothed. "This is one hell of a pickle, but nothing we can't manage."

"Did...you...call...a doctor?" she asked.

A doctor? Why hadn't he acted on that thought back when he'd had it himself? Maybe because he'd figured it would be futile. More likely, because his brain cells had shut down hours ago just the way he'd wanted them to.

"Next thing on my list," he assured her.

She eyed him doubtfully. "You . . . have . . . a list?"

"Of course I have a list," he said, injecting a confident note into his voice. "The water's boiling. The coffee's on."

"Coffee?"

"For me. You don't want me falling asleep in the middle of all the fun, do you?"

"I doubt there's much chance of that," she said, sighing as the pain visibly eased.

Her gaze traveled over him from head to toe, examining him so intently that it was all Luke could do not to squirm. Under other circumstances, that examination would have made his pulse buck so hard he wouldn't have recovered for days. As it was, he looked away as fast as he could. Obviously, this was some sort of penance dreamed up for his sins. He was going to be stranded with Jessie, forced to deliver his brother's baby, and then he was going to have to watch the two of them walk out of his life. Unless, of course . . .

"Luke, can I ask you a question?"

He was relieved by the interruption. There was only heartache in the direction his thoughts were taking. "Seeing how we're going to be getting pretty intimate here in a bit, I suppose you can ask me anything you like."

"Are you drunk?"

He had hoped she hadn't noticed. "Darlin', I don't think you want to know the answer to that."

This time he doubted Jessie's groan of anguish had anything to do with her labor pains.

"Luke?"

"Yes, Jessie."

"Maybe you'd better bring me a very big glass of whatever it was you were drinking."

He grinned at the wistful note in her voice. "Darlin', when this baby turns up, you and I are going to drink one hell of a toast. Until then, I think maybe we'd both better stay as far away from that bottle as we can. Besides, as best I can recall, I smashed it against the fireplace."

She regarded him with pleading blue eyes. "Luke, please? I'm not sure I can do this without help. There's bound to be another bottle of something around here."

He thought of the cabinet filled with whiskey, considered getting a couple of shots to help both of them, then dismissed the temptation as a very bad idea. "You've got all the help you could possibly need. I'm right here with you. Besides, alcohol's not good for the baby. Haven't you read all those headlines warning about that very thing?"

"I don't think the baby's going to be inside me long enough to get so much as a sip," she said.

As if to prove her point, her body was seized with another contraction. Going with sheer instinct, Luke reached out and placed his hand over her taut belly. The skin was smooth and tight as a drum as he massaged it gently until the muscles relaxed.

He checked his watch, talked to her, and waited for the next contraction. It came three minutes later.

He wiped her brow. "Hang in there, darlin'. I'll be right back."

She leveled a blue-eyed glare on him. "Don't you dare leave me," she commanded in a tone that could have stopped the D-Day invasion.

"I'm not going far. I just want some nice, sterile water in here when the baby makes its appearance. And we could use a blanket." And something to cut the umbilical cord, he thought as his brain finally began to kick in without prodding.

He'd never moved with more speed in his life. He tested the phone and discovered the lines were down. No surprise in this weather. He sterilized a basin, filled it with water, then cleaned the sharpest knife he could find with alcohol. He deliberately gave a wide berth to the cabinet with the whiskey. He was back in the bedroom before the next pain hit.

"See there. I didn't abandon you. Did you take natural childbirth classes?"

Jessie nodded. "Started two weeks ago. We'd barely gotten to the breathing part."

"Then we're in great shape," he said with confidence. "You're going to come through this like a champ." The truth was he was filled with admiration for her. He'd always known she had more strength and courage than most women he'd known, but tonight she was proving it in spades.

"Did you call a doctor?" she asked again.

"I tried. I couldn't get through. Don't let it worry you, though. You're doing just fine. Nature's doing all the work. The doctor would just be window dressing."

Jessie shot him a baleful look.

"Okay," he admitted. "It would be nice to have an expert on hand, but this baby's coming no matter who's coaching it into the world, so we might just as well count our blessings that you got to my house. What were you doing out all alone on a night like this anyway?"

"Going to your parents' house," she said. "They invited me for the holidays."

Luke couldn't believe that they'd allowed her to drive this close to the delivery of their first grandchild. "Why the hell didn't Daddy fly you over?"

"He offered. I'm not crazy about flying in such a little plane, though. I told him the doctor had forbidden it."

Luke suspected that was only half the story. He grinned at her. "You sure that was it? Or did that streak of independence in you get you to say no, before you'd even given the matter serious thought?"

A tired smile came and went in a heartbeat. "Maybe."

He hitched a chair up beside the bed and tucked her hand in his. He would not, *would not* allow himself to think about how sweet it was to be sitting here with her like this, despite the fact that only circumstance had forced them together.

"Can't say that I blame you," he said. "If you don't kick up a fuss with Daddy every now and then, next thing you know he's running your life."

"Harlan just wants what's best for his family," she said.

Luke smiled at her prompt defense of her father-in-law. One thing about Jessie, she'd always been fair to a fault. She'd even told anyone who'd listen that she didn't blame him for Erik's death, even with the facts staring her straight in the face. It didn't matter. He'd blamed himself enough for both of them.

"Dad's also dead certain that he's the only one who knows what's best," he added. "Sometimes, though, he misses the mark by a mile."

Her gaze honed in on him. "You're talking about Erik, aren't you? You're thinking about how your father talked him into staying in ranching. If Harlan had let him go, maybe he'd still be alive."

And if Luke had been on that tractor, instead of his brother, Erik would be here right now, he thought. He'd known Erik couldn't manage the thing on the rough terrain, but he'd sent him out there, anyway. He'd told him to grow up and do the job or get out of ranching if he couldn't hack it. Guilt cut through him at the memory of that last bitter dispute.

He glanced at Jessie. The mention of Erik threw a barrier up between them as impenetrable as a brick wall. For once, Luke was glad when the next contraction came. And the next. And the one after that. So fast now, that there was no time to think, no time to do anything except help Jessie's baby into the world.

"Push, darlin'," Luke coaxed.

Jessie screamed. Luke cursed.

"Push, dammit!"

"You don't like how I'm doing it, you take over," she snapped right back at him.

Luke laughed. "That's my Jessie. Sass me all you like, if it helps, but push! Come on, darlin'. I'm afraid this part here is entirely up to you. If I could do it for you, I would."

"Luke?"

There was a plaintive, fearful note in her voice that brought his gaze up to meet hers. "What?"

"What if something goes wrong?"

"Nothing is going to go wrong," he promised. "Everything's moved along right on schedule so far, hasn't it?"

"Luke, I'm having this baby in a ranch house. Doesn't that suggest that the schedule has been busted to hell?"

"Your schedule maybe. Obviously the baby has a mind of its own. No wonder, given the way you take charge of your life. You're strong and brave and your baby's going to be just exactly like you," he said reassuringly.

"I think I've changed my mind," she said with a note of determination in her voice. "I'm not ready for this. I'm not ready to be a mother. I can't cope with a baby on my own."

Luke laughed. "Too late now. Looks to me like that horse is out of the barn."

Moments later, a sense of awe spread through him at the first glimpse of the baby's head, covered with dark, wet hair.

"My God, Jessie, I can see the baby. Just a little more work, darlin', and you'll have a fine, healthy baby in your arms. That's it. Harder. Push harder."

"I can't," she wailed.

"You can," Luke insisted. "Here we go, darlin'." He slid his hands under the baby's tiny shoulders. "One more." Jessie bore down like a trooper and the baby slipped into his hands.

"Luke," Jessie whispered at once. "Is the baby okay? I don't hear anything."

The baby let out a healthy yowl. Luke beamed at both of them. "I think that's your answer," he said.

He surveyed the squalling baby he was holding. "Let's see now. Ten tiny fingers. Ten itsy-bitsy toes. And the prettiest, sassiest blue eyes you ever did see. Just like her mama's."

"Her?" Jessie repeated. She struggled to prop herself up to get a look. "It's a girl?"

"A beautiful little angel," he affirmed as he cleaned the baby up, wrapped her in a huge blanket and laid her in Jessie's arms.

Even though her eyes were shadowed by exhaustion, even though her voice was raspy from screaming, the sight of her daughter brought the kind of smile to Jessie's face that Luke had doubted he would ever see again.

She looked up at him, her eyes filled with gratitude and warmth, and his heart flipped over. A world of forbidden possibilities taunted him.

"She is beautiful, isn't she?" Jessie said, her gaze locked on the tiny bundle in her arms.

"Just about the most gorgeous baby I've ever seen," he agreed, thinking how desperately he wished he could claim her as his own. His and Jessie's. He forced the thought aside. "Do you have a name picked out?"

"I thought I did," she said. "But I've changed my mind."

"Oh? Why is that?"

"Because she rushed things and decided to come at Christmas," she explained. "I'm going to call her Angela. That way I'll always remember that she was my Christmas miracle." She turned a misty-eyed gaze on Luke. "Thank you, Lucas."

If he lived a hundred years, Luke knew he would trade everything for this one moment out of time.

Later the guilt and recriminations would come back with a vengeance. Jessie would remember who he was and what he had done to ruin her life. The blame, no matter how hard she denied it, would be there between them.

But right now, for this one brief, shining moment, they were united, a part of something incredibly special that he could hold in his heart all the rest of his lonely days. They had shared a miracle.

Chapter Three

Jessie felt as if she'd run a couple of marathons back-to-back, but not even that bone-weary exhaustion could take away the incredible sense of joy that spread through her at the sight of her daughter sleeping so peacefully in her arms. Her seemingly healthy baby girl. Her little angel with the lousy sense of timing.

For perhaps the dozenth time since dawn had stolen into the room, bathing it in a soft light, she examined fingers and toes with a sense of amazement that anyone so small could be so perfect. Her gaze honed in on that tiny bow of a mouth, already forming the instinctive, faint smacking sounds of hunger even as she slept. Any minute now she would wake up and demand to be fed.

"Luke, she's hungry," Jessie announced with a mixture of awe and pride that quickly turned to worry. Not once during all the hours of labor or since had she given a single thought to what happened next. "What'll we do?"

Given their past history, it was amazing how quickly she'd come to rely on Luke, how easily she'd pushed aside all of her anger and grief just to make it through this crisis. And, despite his less than alert state on her arrival, despite all the reasons he had for never wanting to see her again, he hadn't let her down yet.

Of course, judging from the way he was sprawled in the easy chair in a corner of the bedroom with his eyes closed, the last bit of adrenaline that had gotten him through the delivery had finally worn off.

Faint, gray light filtered through the frosted window and cast him in shadows. She studied him surreptitiously and saw the toll the past months—or some mighty hard drinking—had taken on him.

The lines that time and weather had carved in his tanned, rugged face seemed deeper than ever. His jaw was shadowed by a day or more's growth of beard. His dark brown hair, which he'd always worn defiantly long, swept the edge of his collar. He looked far more like a dangerous rebel than the successful Texas rancher he was.

If he looked physically unkempt, his clothes were worse. His plaid flannel shirt was clean but rumpled, as if he'd grabbed it from a basket on his way to the door. It was unevenly buttoned and untucked, leaving a mat of dark chest hair intriguingly visible. The jeans he'd hauled on were dusty and snug and unbuttoned at the waist.

Jessie grinned as her gaze dropped to his feet. He had on one blue sock. The other foot was bare. She found the sight oddly touching. Clearly he'd never given a thought to himself all during the night. He'd concentrated on her and seeing to it that Angela made it safely into the world. She would never forget what he'd done for her.

"Luke?" she repeated softly.

The whisper accomplished what her intense scrutiny had not. His dark brown eyes snapped open. "Hmm?" He blinked. "Everything okay?"

"The baby's hungry. What'll we do?"

"Feed her?" he suggested with a spark of amusement.

"Thanks so much." She couldn't keep the faint sarcasm from her voice, but she smiled as she realized how often during the night she'd caught a rare teasing note in Luke's manner. In all the time she'd lived with Erik she'd never seen that side of Luke. He'd been brusque more often than not, curt to the point of rudeness. His attitude might have intimidated her, if she hadn't seen the occasional flashes of something lost and lonely in his eyes. In the past few hours, she'd seen another side of him altogether—strong, protective, unflappable. The perfect person to have around in a crisis. The kind of man on whom a woman could rely.

"Anytime," he teased despite her nasty tone.

Once again he'd surprised her, causing her to wonder if the quiet humor had always been there, if it had simply been overshadowed by his brothers' high spirits.

Still, Jessie was in no mood for levity, as welcome a change as it was. "Luke, I'm serious. She's going to start howling any second now. I can tell. And this diaper you cut from one of your old flannel shirts is sopping. We can't keep cutting up your clothes every time she's wet."

"I have shirts I haven't even taken out of their boxes yet," he said, making light of her concern for his wardrobe. "If I lose a few, it's for a good cause. Besides, I think she looks festive in red plaid."

As he spoke, he approached the bed warily, as if suddenly uncertain if he had a right to draw so close. He touched the baby's head with his fingertips in a caress so gentle that Jessie's breath snagged in her throat.

"As for her being hungry, last I heard, there was nothing better than a mama's own milk for a little one," he said, his gaze fixed on the baby.

"I wasn't planning on nursing her," Jessie protested. "It won't work with the job I have. She'll have to be with a sitter all day. I need bottles, formula." She moaned. There were rare times—and this was one of them—when she wondered how she would cope. She'd counted on Erik to be there for her and the baby. Now every decision, every bit of the responsibility, was on her shoulders.

"Well, given that she decided not to wait for you to get to a hospital or to arrange for a fancy set of bottles," Luke said, still sounding infinitely patient with her, "I'd say Angela is just going to have to settle for

what's on hand for the time being. Don't you suppose you can switch her to a bottle easily enough?''

"How should I know?'' she snapped unreason-
ably.

Luke's gaze caught hers. "You okay?''

"Just peachy.''

His expression softened. "Aw, Jessie, don't start
panicking now. The worst is over.''

"But I don't know what to do,'' she countered, unexpectedly battling tears. "I have three more classes to
take just to learn how to breathe right for the delivery, and a whole stack of baby books to read, and I
was going to fix up a nursery.'' She sobbed, "I...I
even...bought the wallpaper.''

Her sobs seemed to alarm him, but Luke stayed
right where he was. Her presence here might be a burden, her tears a nuisance, but he didn't bolt, as many
men might have. Once more that unflappable response calmed Jessie.

"Seems to me you can forget the classes,'' he observed dryly, teasing a smile from her. "As for the
wallpaper, you'll get to it when you can. I doubt Angela will have much to say about the decor, as long as
her bed's warm and dry. And babies were being born
and fed long before anybody thought to write parenting books. If you're not up to nursing her yet, it seems
to me I heard babies can have a little sugar water.''

"How would you know a thing like that?''

"I was trapped once in a doctor's office with only
some magazines on parenting to read.''

His gaze landed on her breasts, then shifted away
immediately. Jessie felt her breasts swell where his gaze

had touched. Her nipples hardened. The effect could have been achieved because of the natural changes in her body over the past twenty-four hours, but she didn't think that was it. Luke had always had that effect on her. A single look had been capable of making her weak in the knees. She had despised that responsiveness in herself. She was no prouder of it now.

"I have a hunch that left to your own devices, the two of you can figure it out," he said. "I'll leave you alone. I've got chores to do, anyway."

He headed for the door as if he couldn't get away from the two of them fast enough. Jessie glanced up at him then and saw that, while his cheeks were an embarrassed red, there was an expression in his eyes that was harder to read. Wistfulness, maybe? Sorrow? Regret?

"You'll holler if you need me?" he said as he edged through the doorway. Despite the offer of help, he sounded as if he hoped he'd never have to make good on it.

"You'd better believe it," she said.

A slow, unexpected grin spread across his face. "And I guess we both know what a powerful set of lungs you've got. I'm surprised the folks on every other ranch in the county haven't shown up by now to see what all the fuss was about."

"A gentleman wouldn't mention that," she teased.

"Probably not," he agreed. Then, in the space of a heartbeat, his expression turned dark and forbidding. "It would be a mistake to think that I'm a gentleman, Jessie. A big mistake."

The warning startled her, coming as it did on the heels of hours of gentle kindness. She couldn't guess why Luke was suddenly so determined to put them back on the old, uneasy footing, especially since they were likely to be stranded together for some time if the snow kept up through the day as it seemed set on doing.

Maybe it was for the best, though. She didn't want to forget what had happened to Erik. And she certainly didn't want to be disloyal to her husband by starting to trust the man who rightly or wrongly held himself responsible for Erik's death. That would be the worst form of betrayal, worse in some ways perhaps than the secret, unbidden responses of her body. Luke had delivered her baby. She might be grateful for that, but it didn't put the past to rest.

"Well, Angela, I guess we're just going to have to make the best of this," she murmured.

Even as she spoke, she wasn't entirely certain whether she was referring to her first fumbling attempt at breast-feeding or to the hours, maybe even days she was likely to spend in Luke's deliberately ill-tempered company. Days, she knew, she was likely to spend worrying over how great the temptation was to forgive him for what he'd done.

An hour later, the chores done, Luke stood in the doorway of his bedroom, a boulder-size lump lodged in his throat as he watched Jessie sleeping. The apparently well-fed and contented baby was nestled in her arms, her tiny bottom now covered in bright blue plaid. Erik's baby, he reminded himself sharply, when longing would have him claiming her—claiming both of them—for his own.

Sweet Jesus, how was he supposed to get through the next few days until the storm ended, the phone lines were up and the roads were cleared enough for him to get word to his family to hightail it over here and take Jessie off his hands? He'd gotten through the night only because he'd been in a daze and because there were so many things to be done that he hadn't had time to think or feel. Now that his head was clear and the crisis was past, he was swamped with feelings he had no right having.

He forced himself to back away from the door and head for his office. He supposed he could barricade himself inside and give Jessie the run of the house. He doubted she would need explanations for his desire to stay out of her path. Now that her baby was safely delivered, she would no doubt be overjoyed to see the last of him.

Last night had been about need and urgency. They had faced a genuine crisis together and survived. In the calm light of today, though, that urgency was past. He could retreat behind his cloak of guilt. Jessie would never have to know what sweet torment the past few hours had been.

He actually managed to convince himself that hiding out was possible as morning turned into afternoon without a sound from his bedroom. He napped on the sofa in his office off and on, swearing to himself that he was simply too tired to climb the stairs to one of the guest suites. The pitiful truth of it was that he wanted to be within earshot of the faintest cry from either Jessie or the baby. A part of him yearned to be the one they depended on.

Shortly before dusk, he headed back to the barn to feed the horses and Chester. The wind was still howling, creating drifts of snow that made the walk laborious. Still, he couldn't help relishing the cold. It wiped away the last traces of fog from his head. He vowed then and there that no matter how bad things got, he would never, ever try to down an entire bottle of whiskey on his own again. The brief oblivion wasn't worth the hangover. And he hoped like hell he never again had to perform anything as important as delivering a baby with his brain clouded as it had been the night before.

He lingered over the afternoon chores as long as he could justify. He even sat for a while, doling out pieces of apple to the goat, muttering under his breath about the insanity of his feelings for a woman so far beyond his reach. Chester seemed to understand, which was more than he could say for himself.

When he realized he was about to start polishing his already well-kept saddle for the second time in a single day, he forced himself back to the house and the emotional dangers inside. Chester, sensing his indecisiveness, actually butted him gently toward the door.

The back door was barely closed behind him when he heard the baby's cries. He stopped in his tracks and waited for Jessie's murmured attempts to soothe her daughter. Instead, the howls only escalated.

Shrugging off his coat and tossing it in the general direction of the hook on the wall, Luke cautiously headed for the bedroom. He found Jessie still sound asleep, while Angela kicked and screamed beside her. Luke grinned. The kid had unquestionably inherited Jessie's powerful set of lungs. Definitely opera singer caliber.

Taking pity on her worn-out mama, he scooped the baby into his arms and carried her into the kitchen. Once there, he was at a loss.

He held the tiny bundle aloft and stared into wide, innocent eyes that shimmered with tears. "So, kid, it looks like it's just you and me for the time being. Your mama's tuckered out. Can't say I blame her. Getting you into the world was a lot of hard work."

The flood of tears dried up. Angela's gaze remained fixed on his face so attentively that Luke was encouraged to go on. "Seems to me that both of us have a lot to learn," he said, keeping his voice low and even, in a tone he hoped might lull her back to sleep. "For instance, I don't know if you were screaming your head off in there because you're hungry or because you're soaking wet or because you're just in need of a little attention."

He patted her bottom as he spoke. It was dry. She blew a bubble, which didn't answer the question but indicated Luke was definitely on the right track.

"I'm guessing attention," he said. "I'm also guessing that won't last. Any minute now that pretty little face of yours is going to turn red and you're going to be bellowing to be fed. Seems a shame to wake your mama up, though. How about we try to improvise?"

Angela waved her fist in what he took for an approving gesture.

"Okay, then. A little sugar water ought to do it." Cradling her in one arm, he ran some water into a pan, added a little sugar and turned on the burner to warm it. Unfortunately, getting it from the saucepan into the baby required a little more ingenuity.

Luke considered the possibilities. A medicine dropper might work. He'd nourished a few abandoned animals that way as a kid, as well as an entire litter of kittens when the mother'd been killed. One glance into Angela's darkening expression told him he was going to have to do better than that and fast.

"Chester," he muttered in a sudden burst of inspiration. When the old goat had wandered into the path of a mean-spirited bull, Luke had wound up nursing him with a baby bottle for months while he recovered. Where the hell had he put the bottle?

Angela whimpered a protest at the delay.

"Shhh, sweetheart. Everything's going to be just dandy," he promised as he yanked open every single cupboard door in the kitchen. Consuela had the whole place so organized that a single old baby bottle should have stood out like a sore thumb. If it was there, though, he couldn't find it, which meant it was probably out in the barn. He couldn't very well take the baby out there looking for it.

"Damn!" he muttered under his breath.

Huge tears spilled down the baby's cheeks. Obviously she sensed that his plan was falling apart. Any second now she was clearly going to make her impatience known with angry, ear-splitting screams.

"Hey," Luke soothed. "Have I let you down yet?"

Spying Consuela's rubber gloves beside the sink, he had another flash of inspiration. He snatched them up, put another pot of water on to boil, then tossed the gloves in to sterilize them. He found a sewing kit in a drawer, extracted a needle and tossed that in as well.

So far, so good, he reassured himself. The problem came when he judged everything to be sterile. He couldn't poke a hole in one of the glove's fingers and then fill it with warm water while still holding the baby. He grabbed a roasting pan that looked to be about the right size, padded it with a couple of clean dish towels and settled the baby onto the makeshift bed. Judging from the shade of red that her face turned, she was not happy about being abandoned.

"It's only for a minute," he promised her as he completed the preparations by tying a bit of string tightly around the top of the glove. He eyed the water-filled thumb of the glove with skepticism, waiting for the contents to gush out, but it appeared the hole he'd made was just right. He held it triumphantly where Angela could see it. "There! Now didn't I tell you we could manage this? We're a hell of a team, angel."

He picked her up, then sank onto one of the hard kitchen chairs and offered her the improvised bottle. Her mouth clamped on it eagerly and within seconds she was sucking noisily. Luke regarded her with pride.

"You are brilliant," he applauded. "Absolutely the smartest baby ever born."

"You're pretty smart yourself," a sleepy—and damnably sexy—voice commented.

Luke's heart slammed against his ribs. He refused to look up, refused to permit himself so much as a single glance at the tousled hair or bare legs or full, swollen breasts he'd dreamed about too many times to count.

Unfortunately Jessie pulled out a chair smack in his line of vision. She was still wearing his shirt, which came barely to mid-thigh. Her shapely legs were in full view. How many times had he envisioned those legs clamped around him as he made love to her? Enough to condemn his spirit to eternal hell, no doubt about it.

"Feeling rested?" he inquired huskily, keeping his eyes determinedly on the baby he held.

"Some. When did the baby wake up?"

"About a half hour ago. She was hungry."

"So I see."

He could feel a dull, red flush climbing into his cheeks. "I didn't want to wake you. I figured we could manage. It gave me a chance to test that theory I read. Seems to be working. She likes it."

"I'm impressed."

He stood so suddenly that the makeshift bottle slid from Angela's mouth. She protested loudly. Luke shoved both baby and water into Jessie's arms.

"I have work to do." There was no mistaking the sudden expression of dismay in Jessie's eyes, the flicker of hurt at his harsh tone. He managed to grit out a few more words before fleeing. "Help yourself to whatever you need. I'll be in my office."

"Luke, you don't have to run off," she said quietly.

Something in her tone drew his gaze back to her face. The longing he read there shook him more than anything that had happened so far. "Yes, I do," he said tightly.

"Please, I'd like the company."

"No." He practically shouted the word as he bolted.

Her expression stayed with him. Had it truly been longing, he wondered to himself when he was safely away from the kitchen, a locked oak door between him and temptation. Surely he'd been mistaken. No sooner had he reached that conclusion than he cursed himself for a fool. Of course, Jessie was yearning for something right now, but not for him.

No, he told himself sternly, that look had been meant for her husband. It was only natural at a time like this that she would be thinking of Erik, missing him, wishing that he were the one beside her as she fed their first precious baby. Luke was nothing more than a poor substitute.

There was only one way he could think of to keep from making another dangerous mistake like that one. He had to stay inside this room with the door securely locked . . . and temptation on the other side of it.

Chapter Four

Unfortunately, temptation didn't seem inclined to stay out of Luke's path. Only one person could be tapping on his office door not an hour after he'd stalked off in a huff and left her all alone with her baby in the kitchen. Since that display of temper obviously hadn't scared her off, he wondered if she'd have sense enough to take the hint and go away if he didn't answer. He waited, still and silent, listening for some whisper of movement that would indicate she'd retreated as he desperately wanted her to do.

"Luke?" Jessie called softly. "Are you asleep?"

Apparently she didn't have a grain of sense, Luke decided with a sigh. "No, I'm awake. Come on in."

She opened the door and stood at the threshold, shifting uneasily under the glare he had to force himself to direct her way. Despite his irritation, he couldn't seem to take his eyes off her.

She'd wound her long hair up into some sort of knot on top of her head, but it threatened to spill down her back at any second. Luke stared at it in fascination, wondering what she'd do if he helped it along, if he tangled his fingers in those silky strands and tugged her close. An image of their bodies entwined flashed in his head with such vivid intensity it left him momentarily speechless—and racked with guilt.

"Are you hungry?" she asked quietly, ignoring the lack of welcome. "I've fixed enough supper for both of us. I hope you don't mind."

Luke thought of all the reasons he should reject the gesture. If not that, then tell her to bring the food to him in his office. Sharing a meal seemed like a lousy idea. He had no business sitting down across from her, making small talk, acting as if they were a couple or even as if they were friends. Every contact reminded him of the feelings he'd had for her while she'd been married to his brother. Every moment they were in the same room reminded him that those feelings hadn't died. He owed it to her— to both of them—to keep his distance.

Just when he planned to refuse her invitation to supper, he caught the hesitancy in her eyes, the anxious frown and realized that Jessie was every bit as uncertain about their present circumstances as he was. There apparently wasn't a lot of protocol for being stranded with the man responsible for a husband's death, especially when those feelings were all tangled up with feeling beholden to him for delivering her baby.

"Give me a minute," he said with a sigh of resignation.

He watched as she nodded, then closed the door. He shut his eyes and prayed for strength. The truth of it was it would take him an hour, maybe even days to be ready for the kind of time he was being forced to spend with his brother's widow. He had only seconds, not enough time to plan, far too much time to panic, to think of all the dangers represented by having Jessie in his home.

As soon as he'd gathered some semblance of composure, he got to his feet, gave himself a stern lecture about eating whatever she'd fixed in total, uncompromising silence, and then racing hell-bent for leather back to the safety of his den. That decided, he set out to find her.

When he reached the kitchen, where she'd chosen to serve the dinner on the huge oak table in front of a brick fireplace that Consuela had persuaded him to build, the first words out of his mouth were, "I don't want you waiting on me while you're here."

It was hardly a gracious comment, but he had to lay down a few rules or it would be far too easy to fall into a comfortable pattern that would feed all the emotions that had been simmering in him for years now.

She leveled her calm, blue-eyed gaze on him. "We both have to eat. It's no more trouble to fix for two people than it is for one," she said as she dished up a heaping spoonful of mashed potatoes. She passed the bowl to him.

Luke didn't have an argument for that that wouldn't sound even more ungracious than he'd already been, so he kept his mouth clamped shut and his attention focused on the food. The potatoes were creamy with milk and butter. The gravy was smooth and flavored with beef stock, just the way he liked it. The chicken fried steak was melt-in-the-mouth tender. The green beans had been cooked with salt pork.

"When did you have time to do all this?" he asked. He studied her worriedly, looking for signs of exhaustion. She looked radiant. "You're not even supposed to be on your feet yet, are you?"

"There wasn't much to do. Consuela saw to most of it. I've never seen so many little prepackaged, home-cooked meals. She must have been stocking your freezer for a month. How long is she going to be gone, anyway? Or has she abandoned you for good, because of your foul temper?"

"I wouldn't blame her if she had, but no." Luke allowed himself a brief, rueful grin. "She figured company might be dropping by during the holidays, but I doubt she imagined it happening quite this way."

"Neither did you, I suspect." Jessie's penetrating gaze cut right through him. "You'd holed up in here for the duration, hadn't you? You were planning to spend the holidays with your buddy Jack Daniel's." She gestured toward the cabinets. "I saw your supply."

Luke winced at the direct hit. "I've only touched one bottle and I smashed it halfway through," he said defensively.

"Too bad you didn't do it sooner," she observed.

"If I'd known you—and especially Angela—were coming, I would have."

"Now that we are here, what happens next?"

He regarded her cautiously. "What's your real question, Jessie? You might as well spit it out."

Her glance went back to the cabinet. "Are you planning to finish off the rest?"

"Not unless I'm driven to it," he said pointedly.

This time Jessie winced. "Believe me, I know what an imposition this is. We'll be out of your hair as soon as the roads are passable." She glanced toward the windows, where the steadily falling snow was visible. "When do you suppose that will be?"

Luke shrugged. "Don't know. I haven't heard a weather report."

"Are the phones still out?"

"Haven't tried 'em since last night."

"Don't you have a cellular phone? That ought to be working."

To be perfectly honest, Luke hadn't given his cellular phone a thought. He still wasn't used to carrying the damned thing around with him. Keeping track of it was a nuisance. It was probably outside on the seat of his pickup. "I'll check next time I have to go to the barn."

"I could get it. I need to get the rest of my clothes from my car."

Luke cursed himself for not thinking of that. Of course, she'd had luggage with her if she'd been intending a stay at White Pines for the holidays.

"I'll get 'em," he said, pushing away from the table, leaving most of his food uneaten. The excuse was just what he needed to escape this pleasure-pain of sitting across from her in a mockery of a normal relationship between a man and a woman.

"Finish your supper first."

"I'm not hungry," he lied. "I'll get something later. Besides, I'm sure you're anxious to call the folks with the good news. They'll be thrilled to know that you and Erik have a daughter. Doubt they'll be quite so thrilled to hear where you had it though. Dad will want to fly in a specialist to check you and the baby out. He'll probably have a med-evac copter in here before the night's out."

Though he couldn't quite keep the bitterness out of his tone, Jessie grinned at his assessment. "He probably will, won't he? But not even Harlan Adams can defy nature. Nobody's going to be taking off or landing in this blizzard."

"They will if Daddy pays them enough," Luke retorted dryly.

"Well, I won't have it," Jessie retorted with a familiar touch of defiance. "Nobody needs to risk a life on my account. The baby and I are perfectly fine here with you and I intend to tell Harlan exactly that."

Luke had to admire the show of gumption. Obviously, though, Jessie hadn't had to stand up to his father when he got a notion into his head. To save her the fight she couldn't win, he found himself saying, "Maybe it would be best not to make that call, then."

Jessie actually looked as if she was considering it. "But they'll be worried sick about me not showing up last night," she said eventually. "I have to let them know I'm okay."

So, reason had prevailed after all. Luke was more disappointed than he cared to admit.

"Darlin', they've seen the weather," he said, beginning a token and quite probably futile argument, one he had no business making in the first place. Perversity kept him talking, though. "Their phone lines are probably down, too. They'll understand that you probably had to stop along the way and can't get through to let them know."

"Not five seconds ago you were telling me I didn't know your daddy. Now who's kidding himself? Harlan probably has a search party organized. The Texas Rangers are probably out on full alert, sweeping the highways for signs of my car."

There was no denying the truth of that. Luke stood. "Then I suppose we'd better head them off at the pass. I'll get the phone."

He grabbed his heavy sheepskin jacket from the peg by the back door, realizing as he did that Jessie must have hung it there. As he recalled, he'd merely tossed it in that general direction when he'd heard the baby crying earlier. As he pulled it on, he could almost feel her touch. He imagined there was even the faint, lingering scent of her caught up in the fabric.

Outside, the swirling snow and bitter cold cleared his head and wiped away the dangerous sense of cozy familiarity he'd begun to feel sitting at that old oak table with Jessie across from him. He took his time getting Jessie's belongings from her car, then lingered a little longer in the cab of his truck.

As he'd suspected, the cellular phone was on the passenger seat. All he had to do was pick it up and dial home. There wasn't a doubt in his mind that his father would find some way to get Jessie out of his hair before dawn. He would be alone again and safe.

Christmas was only three days away, New Year's a week after that. Surely he could get through so few days without resorting to his original plan of facing them stinking drunk. And heaven knew, Jessie would be better off with his family where the celebrations would be in high gear despite the weather, despite his family's private mourning, where there would be dozens of people to fuss over Angela.

Feeling downright noble about the sacrifice he was making, he actually managed to pick up the phone. But when it came to dialing it, he couldn't bring himself to do it. He thought of the incredible, once-in-a-lifetime miracle he and Jessie had shared. He remembered how it had felt to hold Angela in his arms, to have those trusting, innocent eyes focused on him. Jessie and Angela's unexpected presence had been a gift from a benevolent God, who apparently didn't think his soul was beyond repair.

Would it be so wrong to steal a few more hours, maybe even a day or two with Jessie and Angela? Who could possibly be hurt by it?

Not Erik. He was way past being hurt by anything, not even the knowledge that his brother coveted his widow.

Not Jessie, because Luke would never in a million years act on the feelings she stirred in him.

Not the baby. There was no way he would ever allow anything or anyone to harm that precious child. His paternal instincts, which he'd not even been aware he possessed, had kicked in with the kind of vengeance that made a man reassess his entire existence.

So the only person who might be harmed by his deception would be himself. He stood to lose big time by pretending for even the briefest of moments that Jessie and Angela were a part of his life. Emotions he'd squelched with savage determination were already sneaking past his defenses. The mere fact that he was considering hiding the cellular phone was proof of that.

And yet, he couldn't bring himself to let them go just yet. He'd fallen for Angela as hard as he'd fallen for her mother. Looking into those big blue eyes, he'd felt a connection as strong and powerful as anything he'd ever felt before in his life. He couldn't sever it, not until he understood it.

Likewise, he couldn't watch Jessie disappear until he had finally processed this terrible hold she had on him. From the moment he'd set eyes on her, he'd been riveted. If a bolt of lightning had struck him at that instant, he doubted he would have noticed.

Over time he'd grown to admire her sharp wit, bask in her sensitivity, but in that first instant there had been only a gut-deep attraction unlike anything he'd ever experienced before or since. She had the same effect on him now. He was a man of reason. Surely he could analyze their relationship with cold, calculating logic and finally put it to rest.

He gripped the phone a little tighter and glanced around at the drifts of snow that were growing deeper with each passing minute. A quick toss and no one would find the sucker before spring.

Just as he was about to act on his impulse, that reason of which he was so proud kicked in. What if there was a genuine emergency? The cellular phone might be their only link to the outside world. Instead of burying it in snow, he tucked it into the truck's glove compartment, behind the assortment of maps and grain receipts and who-knew-what-else had been jammed in there without thought. Then he turned the lock securely and glanced guiltily back at the house, wondering if Jessie would guess that he was deliberately keeping her stranded, wondering what her reaction would be if she did know.

Even through the swirling snow, he could see the smoke rising from the chimney, the lights beckoning from the windows. An unexpected sense of peace stole over him. Suddenly, for the first time since he'd built it simply to make a statement to his father—a declaration of independence from Harlan Adams and his need to maintain a tight-fisted control over his sons— the huge, far-too-big monster of a house seemed like a home.

Jessie couldn't imagine what was taking Luke so long. Surely Luke hadn't lost his way in the storm. Though the snowfall was still steady, it was nowhere near as fierce and blinding as it had been.

And he knew every acre of his land as intimately as he might a woman. His voice low and seductive, he'd boasted often enough of every rise and dip, every verdant pasture. He'd done it just to rile his father with his independence, but that didn't lessen the depth of his pride or his sensual appreciation for the land. No,

Luke wasn't lost, which meant he was dallying intentionally.

While he was taking his sweet time about getting back, she was tiring quickly. The last burst of adrenaline had long since worn off. She had already cleaned up the remains of the supper they'd barely touched, washed the dishes and put them away. For the past five minutes she'd been standing at the backdoor, peering into the contrasting world of impenetrable black and brilliant white.

She thought she could see Luke's shadow in the truck and wondered for a moment if he had a bottle stashed there. That array she'd found in his cupboard had worried her. She had never known him to take more than a social drink or two before, had never seen him as on-his-butt drunk as he'd been the night before when she'd arrived.

When at last he climbed out of the truck and headed for the house, she watched his progress with a critical eye. He didn't seem to be staggering, no more so than anyone would be in the deep snow. Shivering at the blast of frigid air, she nonetheless planted herself squarely in the middle of the open doorway, so he couldn't pass by without her getting a whiff of his breath.

"Everything okay?" she called as he neared.

"Fine. Get back inside before you freeze."

Jessie didn't budge. "You took so long I got worried."

He brushed past her, bringing the fresh scent of snow and the tingle of icy air into the house with him. There was no telltale trace of liquor mingling with the crisp winter aromas. She sighed with relief as she closed the door tightly against the night.

"Couldn't find the phone," he announced as he plunked her bags in the middle of the floor. "I'm always forgetting it someplace or another. It'll turn up."

Jessie regarded him suspiciously. His tone seemed a little too hearty. "What about a CB? You must have one and I know your folks do."

"Mine's on the fritz. Haven't seen any reason to get it fixed since I got the phone."

He was deliberately avoiding her gaze. "Luke?" she began quizzically.

He glanced her way for the briefest of seconds. "What?"

Jessie debated calling him on what she suspected were a series of lies, then chastised herself for being far too suspicious. What possible motive would he have for lying? There wasn't a doubt in her mind that he wanted her gone just as badly as she wanted to go. Getting him to the dinner table hadn't been easy. Getting him to stay there had been impossible. He'd seized the first excuse he could to escape. Obviously he wasn't anxious to close the gap that had formed between them when Erik had died on this very ranch.

Last night's emergency and Luke's gentle, caring response to it had been an aberration brought on by extraordinary circumstances. Now they were back to the status quo. She couldn't help the vague feeling of disappointment that stole through her.

Finally she shook her head. "Nothing. I'll take my things to the bedroom." She glanced at him. "Or would you rather I take them to one of the guest suites upstairs?"

Luke seemed unduly angered by the question. "I can take them and you'll stay in the room you're in now."

"But there's no reason for me to put you out of your own room, when there are bedrooms galore upstairs." Left unspoken was the fact that every time she thought about having delivered her baby not simply in Luke's house, but in his bed, an odd sensation stirred in the pit of her stomach. It was a sensation that wouldn't bear too close a scrutiny.

Luke's jaw took on the stubborn set that was a family trait. Erik had been equally bullheaded, his chin perpetually at the same defiant tilt. Yet Erik had been easily swayed, easily reasoned with. Luke, to the contrary, was no pushover.

"Jessie, you'll stay downstairs for as long as you're here," he insisted. "You won't have to climb stairs."

"But I'll be in your way," she protested.

His gaze settled on her. "You won't be in my way," he said with soft emphasis. "This is the way I want it."

She retreated from the argument she clearly had no way of winning. It was his house. She'd stay where he wanted her. "I'll be going to my room, then."

Before she could reach for her bags, Luke shot her a warning look, then picked them up and preceded her down the hall. Inside the room with its dark wood and masculine decor, he deposited the suitcases, then whirled to leave, practically colliding with her in his haste. Jessie's hands immediately went out to steady herself, landing on his chest. Luke jerked as if he'd been brushed by a branding iron. Their gazes clashed, then caught.

"Sorry," she murmured, pulling her hands away.

"Are you okay?"

"You just startled me when you turned around so fast. I stumbled a bit, that's all."

Luke shook his head ruefully. "I'm not used to having to watch out for other people underfoot. It's one of the habits that comes from living alone. Well, not alone exactly. Consuela's here, but she's used to dodging me. To hear her tell it, I've got all the grace of a bull in a china shop. Did I tell you she went to visit her family in Mexico?"

Listening to him, Jessie couldn't stop the smile that tugged at the corners of her mouth. "Lucas, you're babbling," she teased. "Are you nervous for some reason?"

"Nervous?" he repeated the word as if he were testing it. "What would I have to be nervous about?"

"That's what I was wondering. It's not as if we're strangers." Jessie blushed despite herself. "Especially after last night."

A dull red flush crept up Luke's neck. "Maybe it would be best if we didn't talk too much about last night."

"But what you did for me . . ." She tried to think of the right words to express her gratitude.

"I did what anybody would have under the circumstances."

"That's not true. Luke, if you hadn't been here, if you hadn't been who you are . . ."

"Who I am? You mean Erik's brother," he said on an odd, flat note.

"No," she said emphatically. "I mean the kind of man you are, completely unflappable, gentle, competent." She trembled when she thought of the tragedy his presence and his calm, quick actions had averted. "My God, Luke, you delivered my daughter, and if you were even half as terrified as I was, you never let on to me."

"Try three or four times as terrified," he corrected. "I just talked a good game."

Jessie reached up and rested her hand against his stubbled cheek, felt a faint shudder whisper through him, saw his eyes darken. "Don't joke," she chided. "I'm serious. I'm trying to thank you properly for what you did, for bringing my baby safely into the world. I'll never forget it."

"There's no need for thanks," he said, brushing aside her gratitude.

"There is," she insisted, trying to think of an adequate way of showing him how grateful she was. The perfect gesture suddenly came to her and she blurted it out impulsively, not pausing to think of the implications. "In fact, I would be honored if you would consider being Angela's godfather. I know that's what Erik would have wanted, too."

Luke's eyes turned cold and he broke away from her touch. "You're wrong, if you think that," he said flatly. "I'm the last man in the world Erik would want anywhere near you or your daughter."

Too late, Jessie realized she couldn't have shattered the quiet moment any more effectively if she'd tossed a live hand grenade into the room. By mentioning Erik, by reminding Luke of his brother, she had destroyed their fragile accord.

"Luke, that's not true..." she began, but she was talking to herself. Luke had fled from the room as if he'd just been caught committing a crime and a posse of lawmen were after him, guns already blazing.

Troubled, Jessie stared after him. Not until she heard her daughter whimper did she move. Picking Angela up from her makeshift bed, a blanket-lined drawer, she paced the floor with her until she quieted.

"You know something, angel? Your Uncle Luke is a very complicated, perplexing man."

No one knew more clearly than she did how dangerous those two traits could be in a man, especially for a woman who enjoyed nothing more than solving puzzles.

Chapter Five

There was a huge stack of unpaid bills on Luke's desk. Normally he hated sitting there with a calculator, checking the totals against his own records, writing the checks, meticulously balancing the books. The process bored him. The mistakes irritated him. If he'd wanted to do this much math, he'd have been a damned accountant.

Tonight, though, the tedium of the assignment drew him. In fact, he hadn't been able to leave that bedroom fast enough to get to his office and shut the door behind him. Only a vague sense of the absurdity of the action kept him from bolting it.

At any rate, as long as he had to concentrate on numbers written out in black and white, numbers that either added up or didn't, he wouldn't have to think about the woman in his bedroom who made no sense to him at all.

What had possessed Jessie to suggest that he be godfather to Angela? Couldn't she see how inappropriate that was? Couldn't she guess how deeply hurt the rest of the family would be over her choice? Hell, they probably wouldn't even show up for the baptism. They'd be certain she'd placed the baby's very soul in jeopardy by selecting her father's killer as the baby's godparent.

Okay, she was grateful for his help in delivering the baby. He could understand that. He didn't think thanks were necessary, but if Jessie did, she could have found a dozen ways of thanking him that wouldn't turn the entire family inside out. A framed snapshot of the baby would have sufficed. A dutiful note would have covered it.

Instead, with all the impulsiveness and generosity he'd always admired in her, she had made a grand gesture that would have ripped the family apart. They would have chosen sides. In the end, more than likely Jordan and Cody would have backed Jessie's choice. His parents would have been appalled. Even he cared enough for the family's feelings to want to avoid deliberately causing them any more anguish.

Fortunately, his head at least had been clear. He'd said no before she could get too carried away with her planning.

He raked his hand through his hair and muttered an oath under his breath. A tiny part of him regretted the necessity for declining her offer. Being godparent to the baby he'd helped deliver would have bound him to

Jessie and Angela. It would have kept him on the fringes of their lives. It would have placed him where no one would have questioned his involvement, where he could watch out for them.

Where he could torture himself, he added bleakly. Saying no had been the right decision, the only decision.

Determinedly, he picked up the first invoice from the pile on his desk and went to work. Sometime between the first bill and the second, he fell soundly asleep. The next thing he knew it was morning and the very woman who'd been tormenting him in his dreams was hovering around in his office as if she belonged there.

"What the hell are you doing?" he asked crankily, rubbing his aching shoulders as he eyed Jessie warily. For a woman who'd just had a baby less than forty-eight hours before, she was damned energetic. Normally he'd consider that an admirable trait, but at the moment it seemed a nuisance to have her bustling around as if he weren't even there. "Jessie, whatever you're up to, give it a rest."

"I'm getting some light in here. It's dark as pitch." She drew back the draperies with a flick of her wrist, revealing the blinding glare of sunlight on snow.

"Beautiful, isn't it?" she asked cheerfully. "I'll be back in a minute with your breakfast. You really shouldn't sleep at your desk, Lucas. It's bad for your back."

Given the fact that every muscle between his neck and his butt ached like the very dickens, Luke couldn't argue with her. If she hadn't taken off, though, he would have had a few things to say about her intrusion into his domain. He figured they could wait until she returned. If she brought strong, black coffee with her, he might even moderate his protest to a dull roar.

He stood up cautiously, testing to see if any of his parts actually worked. His legs held him upright, which was better than he deserved. He stretched carefully, slowly working the kinks loose. By the time he heard Jessie's returning footsteps, he was feeling almost civilized. That didn't mean he intended to tolerate her sudden burst of uninvited activity.

Unfortunately for his resolve, the aroma of coffee preceded her into the room. Oblivious to whatever order there might be to his desk, she brushed piles of papers aside and deposited a tray laden with pancakes, eggs, bacon and a pot of coffee. Luke glanced at the new disarray, considered bellowing in outrage, then took another whiff of that coffee and poured himself a cup instead. He sipped it gratefully as he sank back into his leather chair.

Maybe the bustling wasn't so bad, after all. Only trouble now was, she didn't go away. In fact, she seemed to be waiting for something. She hovered at the edge of his desk, her gaze fixed on him as if trying to determine how to broach whatever was on her mind.

"Coffee's good," he said, watching her uneasily. "Thanks."

"You're welcome."

"Don't worry about the dishes. I'll bring them back to the kitchen and wash up when I'm done," he said, hoping she'd take the hint and leave.

She actually grinned at that. "Trying to get rid of me?" she inquired.

Almost as if to taunt him, she pulled up a chair and sat down. What astonished him was the fact that even though she was wearing her oversize maternity clothes, she managed to look as sexy as if she'd been wearing something slinky. His imagination was perfectly capable of envisioning every curve under her shapeless top. As if it might make a difference, he turned his attention to the food she'd brought. He poured syrup on the pancakes and cut into the eggs.

"I told you yesterday that I didn't want you waiting on me," he reminded her even as he took his first bite of pancakes. They were light as air. He knew for a fact that Consuela hadn't left these, which meant Jessie had been cooking. "You need to rest. Taking care of a new baby is tiring. I want you concentrating on Angela."

"Angela's fine. She's been fed. Now she's sleeping. That's what newborns do."

He snapped a piece of crisp bacon into crumbs and prayed for patience. "So, rest while you have the chance. Read a book. The library next door is filled with them."

"Maybe later."

He could see he was getting nowhere. Maybe if he divided up the chores and took the lion's share himself, she'd restrict herself to doing only what she'd been assigned.

"Okay, here's the deal," he said. "I'll fix breakfast and lunch. You can deal with supper, since Consuela already has those dishes prepared and ready to pop into the oven. I'll clean up. Agreed?''

"That hardly sounds fair," she said. "I'll cook all the meals. You clean up."

"No," Luke insisted, his voice tight. "We'll do it my way. And since you've already done breakfast today, I'll handle dinner. You're done for the day. Go take a nap."

"I wonder why I never noticed before what a bully you are," she commented, her expression thoughtful.

The observation didn't seem to trouble her a bit, but he found it insulting. "I am not a bully. I'm just trying to divvy things up fairly."

"You have an odd notion of fair," she observed. "Oh, well, never mind. I won't argue for the moment. Maybe you should consider the pancakes a bribe," she suggested.

Luke's gaze narrowed. "A bribe? For what?"

"So you'll do what I want, of course."

"Which is?"

She opened her mouth, seemed to reconsider, then closed it again. "No, I think we'll wait and talk about it later. I think you could use a little more buttering up." She stood and headed for the door.

Luke stared after her in astonishment. "Jessie!"

His bellow clearly caught her by surprise. She halted in the doorway and looked back. The glance she shot him couldn't have been more innocent if she'd been a newborn baby.

"Yes?" she said.

"What kind of game are you playing here?"

"No game," she insisted.

"You want something, though. What is it?"

"It can wait. Enjoy your breakfast."

"Tell me now," he ordered.

She smiled. "I don't think so."

She closed the door with quiet emphasis before he could even form another question. Suddenly, despite himself, he found himself laughing.

"Well, I'll be damned," he said aloud. "Maybe I underestimated you, after all, Jessie Adams. Seems to me you have gumption to spare, more than enough to take on the Adams men."

On the other side of the door, Jessie heard the laughter and the comment. "You ain't seen nothing yet, Luke Adams," she murmured sweetly.

Unlocking the puzzle that Luke represented had become a challenge she couldn't resist. And drawing Erik's family back together seemed like the best Christmas gift she could possibly give to all of them. She'd come to that conclusion during a long and restless night.

Erik wouldn't have wanted his death to split them apart. He wouldn't have wanted the unspoken accusations, the guilt and blame to stand between Luke and his parents. Whatever had happened on Luke's ranch that day, Erik would never have blamed the big brother he'd idolized. He would have forgiven him. As much as Erik had craved his independence, he had loved his family more. If he hadn't, he might have fought harder to break free from Harlan's influence.

If, if, if...so many turning points, so many choices made, a few of them deeply regretted.

If she had accepted Harlan's offer to fly to his ranch, then the storm and her unexpected labor wouldn't have forced Jessie into accepting Luke's help and his hospitality. If that wasn't a sign from God, she didn't know what was. Obviously, He had given her a mission here and the most readily accessible place to start was with Luke. After all, Christmas was a time for miracles.

With the snow plows uncertain, she figured she had a few days at least to utilize her powers of persuasion. By the time the roads were cleared, she was determined that she and Angela wouldn't be going on to Harlan and Mary's alone to celebrate the new year and a new beginning. Their son would be with her.

By late that afternoon, Jessie's plans and her temper were frayed. She hadn't seen more than the flash of Luke's shadow the entire day. He'd managed to sneak lunch onto the table and disappear before she could blink. She'd passed his office, just in time to see him vanish into the library. She'd bundled up and trailed him to the barn, only to see him riding away on horseback. A gimpy old goat had been gamely trying to follow him.

Shivering, she had trudged back inside only to hear Angela screaming at the top of her lungs. Nothing she'd done had settled the baby down. Angela was dry and fed. For the past twenty minutes, Jessie had been rocking her in front of the fire in the kitchen. Angela's great, hiccupping sobs continued unabated.

"A few more minutes of this and you'll have me in tears, too," Jessie murmured in distress. "Come on, sweetheart. You're tired. Go off to sleep, like mommy's little angel."

Blessed silence greeted the suggestion. Five seconds later, Angela screamed even louder than before. Obviously she'd only taken time off to rev up her engine.

Jessie could feel the first, faint beginnings of panic. Already uncertain about her mothering skills, her inability to soothe her baby seemed to confirm just how unprepared and inept she was.

Because the rocking seemed to be making both of them more jittery than serene, she stood and began to pace as she racked her brain for some new technique to try.

She tried crooning a lullaby, singing an old rock song at full volume, rubbing her back. She was at her wit's end when she heard the back door slam.

Luke hesitated just inside the threshold. "What's all this racket?" he demanded, but there was a teasing note in his voice and a spark of amusement in his eyes. "I could hear both of you all the way out at the barn. Chester took off for parts unknown. The horses are trying to hide their heads under the hay."

"Very funny," Jessie snapped just as Luke reached for the baby. She relinquished her all too readily.

"Come here, angel," he murmured consolingly. "You were just missing Uncle Luke, weren't you?"

Jessie's traitorous daughter gulped back a sob, then cooed happily. Held in the crook of Luke's arm, she looked tiny, but thoroughly contented. Jessie wanted to warn her that a man's arms weren't a guarantee of protection, but maybe that was a lesson it was too soon to teach. If the feel of Luke's strength could silence the baby's cries for now, Jessie had no complaints. She felt the oddest, most compelling yearning to have his arms around her as well. With her hormones bouncing around in the wake of the baby's birth, she seemed to be more insecure than ever.

Luke glanced her way. "Stop hovering. We're doing fine. I'm going to start supper and Angela's going to help, aren't you, munchkin?"

Jessie sank gratefully onto a kitchen chair and watched Luke's efficient movements as he pulled packages from the freezer with one hand, all the while carrying on a nonsensical conversation with the baby. Jessie sighed with envy as she watched him.

"How do you do that?" she asked.

He shrugged. "Maybe it's like a horse. If it knows you're afraid, it'll buck you off sure thing. If you handle it with confidence, it'll go along with you."

Jessie sorted through the metaphor and came to the conclusion he thought she was scared to death of her own daughter. "In other words, I'm lousy at this."

He shot a glance over his shoulder at her. "Did I say that? I thought I was saying that she senses you're not sure of yourself."

"Well, I'm not."

"You will be."

"How did you get to be so good with babies?"

"Three younger brothers, I suppose. All three of them had very different temperaments. Jordan was the charmer from day one. He could wheedle anything out of anybody. He gurgled and smiled and cooed. Even Daddy wasn't immune to him. It's no wonder he's been such an incredible business success."

"And Cody?"

"He's the flirt. There hasn't been a woman born he couldn't win over. Daddy couldn't handle him worth a lick. Come to think of it, Mama could never handle him either, but he could always make her think she'd won. He wrapped Consuela around his little finger and, believe me, she's no patsy."

"What about Erik? What was he like?" Jessie asked cautiously, keeping her gaze on Luke's face. His expression didn't change, but he did hesitate. For a moment she almost regretted bringing him up.

"Erik was the diplomat," he said eventually. "He was the master of compromise. If Mama gave him two chores, he'd make her settle for one. If Daddy ordered him to be home at midnight, Erik would compromise for twelve-thirty. He never, ever accepted their first offer. If he'd been in the foreign service, it was a skill that would have served him well. As it was, he compromised himself into waiting for the life he really wanted by offering to prove himself first as a rancher."

There was a note of sorrow in his voice that resonated deep inside Jessie. "He wanted so badly to be a teacher in junior high, the age when kids are testing themselves, and he would have been good at it, too," she said. "He just wanted to please your father."

"He should have known that nothing would impress Daddy except success," Luke said bitterly. "If Erik had stuck to his guns and gone on to be a teacher, if he'd won recognition for that, it would have pleased Daddy more than seeing him trying to be a rancher and failing."

Jessie felt a surge of anger on Erik's behalf. "Don't belittle your brother for trying. At least he admitted that he was staying at the ranch in an attempt to gain your father's approval. You won't even admit that's what you're doing." She waved her hand to encompass the kitchen, the whole house. "Isn't that what all of this is for, to impress your father, to prove you could start from scratch, without a dime of his money and have a bigger, more impressive ranch?"

As if she sensed the sudden tension, Angela whimpered. Luke soothed her with a stroke of his finger across her cheek and a murmured, "Shh, angel. Everything's okay. Your mama and I are just having a slight difference of opinion."

His angry gaze settled on Jessie. "I bought this ranch because ranching is what I do. I built this house because I needed a home."

"How many bedrooms, Luke? Five? Seven? More than there are over at White Pines, I'll bet. And how many rooms do you really live in? Two, maybe three, if you don't count the kitchen as Consuela's domain?"

"What's your point?"

"That you're every bit as desperate for approval from Harlan as Erik ever was. You're just determined to do it by besting him at his own game."

"Or maybe I was just planning ahead for the time when I have a family to share this ranch with me," he said quietly, his gaze pinned on her. "Maybe I was thinking about coming in from the cold and finding the woman I loved in front of the fire, holding my baby."

The softly spoken remark, the seductive, dangerous look in his eyes held Jessie mesmerized. His voice caressed her.

"Maybe I was imagining what it would be like when this was no longer just a house, but a home, filled with warmth and laughter and happiness. Or didn't you ever stop to think that I might have dreams?"

"So why don't you do something to turn it into a home?" she taunted before she could stop herself.

The look he shot her was unreadable, but there was something in the coiled intensity of his body language that sent a thrill shimmering straight through her.

"Perhaps I have," he said, his challenging gaze never leaving hers.

Then, while Jessie's breath was still lodged in her throat, he pressed a kiss to the baby's cheek, handed her back to her mother and sauntered from the room with the confidence of a man who'd just emerged triumphant from a showdown at the OK Corral.

That was the last she saw of him until after the supper she'd been forced to eat alone. She'd spent most of the evening the same way, alone in the kitchen, pondering what Luke had said—and what he hadn't. With the radio tuned to Christmas carols, her mood was a mix of nostalgia and wistfulness and confusion.

She hadn't especially wanted to spend the holidays with Erik's family, hadn't been much in the mood for celebrating at all in fact, but now that Christmas was only two days away, she couldn't help thinking of the way it had been the year before. She wondered if she would ever recapture those feelings.

The whole family and dozens of friends had been crowded around a gigantic tree, its branches loaded with perfectly matched gold ornaments and tiny white lights, chosen by a decorator. Mary had played carols on the baby grand piano, while the rest of them sang along, their voices more exuberant than on key.

Jessie remembered thinking of all the quiet Christmases as she'd been growing up, all the times she'd longed for a boisterous houseful of people. With her hand tucked in Erik's, she'd been so certain that for the first time she finally understood the joy of the season. Her heart had been filled to overflowing. In agreeing to go to White Pines this year, perhaps she'd been hoping to reclaim that feeling for herself and eventually for her baby.

It seemed unlikely, though, that it would have been the same. Erik had stolen her right to be there from her, wiped it away in an instant of carelessness that she'd never really doubted for a moment was as much his fault as Luke's. Sometimes, when it was dark and she was scared, she blamed Luke, because it hurt too much to blame her husband.

Everything Luke had said earlier was true. Erik had hated working on the ranch, whether his father's or his brother's. He'd had other dreams, but his father had been too strong and Erik too weak to fight. He'd preferred working for Luke, who tolerated his flaws more readily than his father did. He'd accepted his fate by rushing through chores, by doing things haphazardly, probably in a subconscious bid to screw up so badly that his father or Luke would finally fire him.

Well, he'd screwed up royally, all right, but he'd died in the process, costing both of them the future they'd envisioned, costing Angela a father and her the extended family she'd grown to love. Sometimes Jessie was so filled with rage and bitterness over Erik's unthinking selfishness that she was convinced she hated him, that she'd never loved him at all.

At other times, like now, she regretted to her very core all the lost Christmases, all the lost moments in the middle of the night when they would have shared their hopes and dreams, all the children they'd planned on having.

"Jessie?" Luke said, interrupting her sad thoughts as he stood in the kitchen doorway, his hands shoved in the pockets of his jeans. "Are you okay?"

"Just thinking about last year and how much things have changed," she admitted.

Luke's eyes filled with dismay. "I'm sorry. I know facing a Christmas without Erik is the last thing you expected," he said, regarding her worriedly. "Why don't you come on in the living room? I've started a fire in there."

Without argument Jessie stood and followed him. She was frankly surprised by the unexpected invitation, but she had no desire to spend the rest of the evening alone with her thoughts, even if being with Luke stirred feelings in her that she didn't fully understand.

When Luke stood by the fireplace, Jessie crossed over to stand beside him. He looked so sad, so filled with guilt, an agonizing of guilt that had begun some seven months ago for both of them. Instinctively she reached for him, placing her hand on his arm. The muscle was rigid.

She tried to make things right. "I don't blame you for the way things are, Luke. I wanted to. I wanted to lash out at someone and you were the easiest target. You were there. You could have stopped him." She sighed. "The truth is, though, that Erik was always trying to prove himself, taking chances. You couldn't have kept him off that tractor if you'd tried."

He shrugged off her touch. "Maybe not, but I blame myself just the same. Look what I've cost you."

Jessie wanted to explain that it wasn't Erik she missed so much as the feeling of family that had surrounded them all that night as they sang carols. To say that aloud, though, would be a betrayal of her husband, an admission that their life together hadn't been perfect. She owed Erik better than that. He had given her the one thing she'd never had—the feeling of belonging to a family with history and roots.

"Regrets are wasted, Lucas. We should be concentrating on the here and now. It's almost Christmas, the season of hope and renewal," she said.

She glanced around the living room, which looked as it would at any other time of the year—expensive and sterile. It desperately needed a woman's touch. Even more desperately, it needed to be filled with love.

"You'd never even know it was the holidays in here," she chided him. "There's not so much as a single card on display. I'll bet you haven't even opened them."

"Haven't even been out to the mailbox in days," he admitted.

She lifted her gaze to his. "How can you bear it?" Before he could answer, she shook her head. "Never mind. That was what the cabinet full of liquor was all about, wasn't it?"

"Sure," he said angrily. "It was about forgetting for a few blessed days, forgetting Christmas, forgetting Erik, forgetting the guilt that has eaten away at me every single day since my brother died right in front of my eyes."

Jessie flinched under the barrage of heated words. "Sounds like you've been indulging in more than whiskey. You sound like a man who's been wallowing in self-pity."

"Self-loathing," Luke said.

"Has it made you feel better?" she chided before she could stop herself. She'd been there, done that. It hadn't helped. "Has anything been served by you sitting around here being miserable?"

He didn't seem to have an answer for that. He just stared at her, his expression vaguely startled by her outburst.

"Don't you think I feel guilty sometimes, too?" she demanded. "Don't you think I want to curl up in a ball and bemoan the fact that I lost a husband after only two years of marriage? Well, I do."

She was on a roll now, releasing months of pent-up anger and frustration. She scowled at him. "But I for one do not intend to ruin the rest of my life indulging in a lot of wasted emotions. I cried for Erik. I grieved for him. But a part of him lives on in Angela. I think that's something worth celebrating. Maybe you're content to spend the holidays all shut up in this bleak atmosphere, but I'm not.''

Oblivious to his startled expression, oblivious to everything except the sudden determination to take charge of her life again, starting here and now, she declared, ''The minute I get up tomorrow morning, I am going to make this damned house festive, if I have to make decorations from popcorn and scraps of paper.''

She shot him a challenging look. She had had it with his veiled innuendoes and sour mood. ''As for you, you can do what you damned well please.''

Chapter Six

Sitting right where he was, staring after Jessie long after she'd gone, Luke realized he hadn't given a thought to Christmas beyond being grateful that he wouldn't be spending it with his family, enduring their arguments and silences, their grief. Consuela had dutifully purchased his gifts to everyone, wrapped them and sent them over to White Pines. He'd merely paid the bills.

Now, though, he would have had to be denser than stone to miss Jessie's declaration that the atmosphere around his house was awfully bleak for the season. That parting shot before she'd gone off to her room had been a challenge if ever he'd heard one. Just thinking about it was likely to keep him up half the night, wondering how he could give them both a holiday they would never forget. There was no question in his mind that with Jessie and Angela in the house, it would be wrong, if not impossible, to ignore the holiday—the baby's first.

A week ago he hadn't expected to feel much like celebrating, but for the past forty-eight hours his mood had been lighter than it had been in months. Part of that was due to Angela's untimely, but triumphant, arrival. She was truly a Christmas blessing. A far greater measure of his happiness was due, though, to this stolen time with Jessie and his sense that she truly didn't blame him for Erik's accident.

He finally admitted at some point in the middle of the night that instead of getting her out of his system, he was allowing her to become more firmly entrenched in his heart. He could readily see now that his initial attraction to Jessie had been pure chemistry, tinged with the magical allure of the forbidden. In some ways, his conscience insisted, she was even more out of reach to him now.

But he knew in his gut that the attraction went beyond her being unavailable to him. Traits he'd only suspected before were clear to him now. He was coming to know her strengths and her weaknesses in a whole new way and nothing he'd discovered disappointed him.

In addition to being beautiful and warmhearted, she was also quick-tempered. In addition to being strong and brave, she was also willful and stubborn. She had a quick wit and a ready laugh, but she could also be a bit of a nag when she believed in her cause. In his view the positives outweighed the negatives. The contrariness only made her more interesting.

Those discoveries solidified his long-held belief that she and Erik had been mismatched from the start. As much as he had adored his younger brother, he'd also recognized that Erik was weak, too weak to stand up to their father, too weak to provide much of a challenge to a woman like Jessie.

He'd wondered more than once what had drawn them together in the first place. Observing them in years past with a sort of detached fascination, he had had no problem guessing why Erik had chosen a woman with Jessie's strengths. Less clear was why she had fallen in love with his brother. The past couple of days had given him some insight into that.

He was beginning to realize that far from being the gold digger she had appeared to some distrusting family members at first glance, Jessie had simply craved being part of a family with history and roots. On the surface, anyway, his family was storybook caliber with its strong men, boisterous affection, deeprooted ties to the Texas land and abiding sense of loyalty. Erik had been her passport to all of that.

He couldn't help wondering, though, why she had chosen to move across the state after Erik's death, when she could have stayed at White Pines, claimed her rightful place in the family she'd obviously grown to love, and been doted on.

As he understood it, his parents had begged her to stay, especially after they'd learned she was pregnant. Even though it had meant giving up something desperately important to her, Jessie had insisted on going.

Whatever her reasons, he admired her for standing up to them. He also knew she hadn't taken a dime when she'd left. It was yet more testament to her character, proof that she had married Erik for love, not for money.

Lingering in the barn, Luke was leaning against a stall door, still contemplating Jessie, when Chester butted him from behind. The old goat was obviously tired of being ignored. Luke turned on him with mock indignation.

"Hey, what was that all about? Goats who get pushy don't get treats."

Chester didn't get the message. He nudged Luke's coat pocket trying to get at the sections of apple he knew were there. Luke dug them out and fed them to him.

"So, what do you think, Chester? What can I do to make this holiday special?"

Since the goat didn't seem to have any sage advice, Luke headed back toward the house. He was almost there when inspiration struck. He might not be able to deliver a load of gifts or even an album of Christmas carols, but he could certainly come up with a tree.

He detoured to the woodpile for an ax, then headed into the stand of pine trees on the ridge behind the house. He'd planted most of them up there himself, full-grown pines that had cost a fortune. He supposed he'd done it just because his parents had no similar trees, despite the name of their home. The gesture had been some sort of perverse link to his past.

He surveyed the cluster of trees critically, dismissing several as too scrawny, a few more as misshapen, though they'd all seemed perfect to him when he'd chosen them from the nursery. Finally his gaze landed on a tree that was tall and full and fragrant.

He worked up a sweat and an appetite chopping it down, then dragging it through the snow all the way back to the house. Propped up against the back porch railing, the tree seemed ever-so-slightly larger than it had on the ridge. He eyed it uneasily and decided he might have been just a little optimistic about fitting it into the house. Still, there was no denying that it was impressive. It made a statement, one he hoped that Jessie couldn't mistake.

After stomping the snow off his boots and dusting it from his clothes, he snuck inside to make sure that Jessie was still in bed. During the night as he'd been sitting awake in the living room staring into the fire, he'd heard her pacing the floor with the baby. Hopefully, she was catching up on lost sleep this morning.

He tiptoed down the hall as silently as a man his size could manage, then edged the bedroom door open a crack. Down for the count, he decided, after watching the soft rise and fall of her chest for several seconds more than was entirely necessary.

Angela, however, was another story. In her makeshift bed, a drawer they had lined with blankets, she was cooing to herself and waving her arms as if to let him know she was ready for an adventure. Luke couldn't resist the invitation. There was something about holding that tiny bundle of brand new life in his arms that filled him with a sense of hope.

Swearing to himself that he was only picking the baby up to keep her from waking Jessie, he carried her, bed and all, into the kitchen. Those serious eyes of hers remained fixed on him trustingly all the way down the hall. He was certain they were filled with anticipation, indicating she was ready to try anything. He figured she was destined to break a good many hearts with what seemed to him her already-evident daredevil nature.

"Now, then, sweet pea, can you be very quiet while I bring the tree in? Just wait till you see it. It's your very first Christmas tree and, if I do say so myself, it's just about the prettiest one I've ever seen."

Angela seemed willing to be temporarily abandoned. Luke was on the porch and back in a flash, lugging the tree through the kitchen and into the living room. He found the perfect spot for it in the nook formed by a huge bay window. As soon as he'd put it down, he went back into the kitchen for the baby. This time he plucked her out of her bed and carried her in his arms, admiring the simple red plaid sleeper Jessie had apparently stitched up from another one of his old shirts.

"So, what do you think?" he asked as he stood before the tree, admiring the sweep of its branches against the ten-foot-high ceiling. Placing it in a stand, assuming he even had one that would fit its thick trunk, definitely would require a little trimming at the top.

Angela seemed fascinated. He echoed her approval. "Pretty awesome, huh? Wait till you see it with lights and decorations. You won't be able to take your eyes off it."

The only problem was the lights, the decorations and the tree stand were all stored upstairs. He had a hunch she wouldn't tolerate being put back in that drawer again. "Now that is a quandary," he said to Angela. "But we can solve it, can't we? I'll just settle you right here on the floor so you can see, put some pillows around you in case you happen to be precocious enough to roll over. I think that's a little advanced even for someone of your brilliance, but there's no point in taking chances."

Angela's face scrunched up the instant he deposited her among the pillows. He propped her up so she had a better view of the tree, an arrangement which seemed to improve her disposition. "Now don't let me down, angel," he cajoled. "No crying, okay? I promise I'll be back before you can say Santa Claus."

He darted worried glances over his shoulder all the way out of the room. The baby seemed to have settled into her nest without a fuss. He doubted her contentment would last, though.

Thankfully, Consuela was the most organized human being he'd ever met. The Christmas decorations were tidily stacked and labeled in a storage closet, where he'd insisted they remain this year. She'd succeeded in sneaking a fat, pine-scented candle and a table decoration into the dining room, but that was all she'd dared after his firm instructions.

Luke managed to get all the boxes into his arms at once, then juggled them awkwardly as he made his way back downstairs. The boxes began to wobble dangerously halfway down. The top one tumbled off, then the one after that. There was no mistaking the tinkling sound of glass breaking. Mixed with his muttered oaths and Angela's first faint whimpers, it was apparently more than enough to wake Jessie.

He'd just turned the corner to the living room when she came staggering out of the bedroom, sleepily swiping at her eyes. "What's going on? Where's Angela?"

Luke stepped in front of her and blocked her view of the living room. "Everything's under control. Why don't you go back to bed? You must be exhausted after being up half the night."

"I'm awake now. What broke?"

"Nothing important."

"What's all that stuff you're carrying?"

"For someone who's half-asleep, you ask a lot of questions. Did you get a job I don't know about as a reporter?"

Ignoring the question, she blinked and took a step closer. Her heavy-lidded gaze studied the boxes. When the contents finally registered, her face lit up with astonishment. "Christmas decorations?"

Luke sighed. So much for his surprise. "Christmas decorations," he confirmed, then shifted out of her way so she could see past him.

"I thought Angela should have a tree for her first Christmas," he admitted sheepishly. "You made it pretty clear last night how you felt about the lack of holiday spirit around here. I decided you were right."

Jessie's eyes widened. "Luke, it's . . ."

"Awesome?" he suggested, after trying to study the tree objectively. Despite the impressive size of the room, the tree took up a significant portion of it.

"Huge," Jessie declared.

"I know. It didn't look nearly as big outside."

Before he realized what she intended, Jessie turned and threw her arms around his neck. "Thank you," she said, kissing him soundly.

Her lips were warm and pliant against his, impossibly seductive. The impulsive gesture almost caused him to drop the remaining boxes. "Jessie!" he protested softly, though there was some doubt in his mind if he was warning her away to save the decorations or his sanity.

She regarded him uncertainly for the space of a heartbeat, but apparently she chose to believe he was worried about the ornaments. She claimed several of the boxes and carried them into the living room. Then she took a thorough survey of the tree and pronounced it the most incredible tree she had ever seen. The glint of excitement in her eyes was enough to make Luke's knees go weak. If she ever directed a look half so ecstatic at him, he could die a happy man.

"Don't do a thing until I get back," she demanded as she headed from the room.

"Where are you going?"

"To get dressed and to make hot chocolate."

He thought she looked exquisite in her robe, a pale pink concoction that was all impractical satin and lace. As for the hot chocolate, he was plenty warm enough as it was. "Not on my account," he said.

"On mine," she said, visibly shivering. "I'm freezing in this robe."

The innocent comment lured him to look for evidence. He found it not in the expected goose bumps, but in the press of hard nipples against the robe's slinky fabric. "I'll turn the heat up," he countered eventually. Anything to keep her in that softly caressing robe.

Apparently she caught the choked note in his voice or the direction of his gaze, because her expression faltered a bit. A delectable shade of pink tinted her cheeks. "It'll only take a minute," she insisted. "Besides, we can't possibly decorate a tree without hot chocolate. I'm pretty sure there's a law to that effect."

Luke found himself grinning at the nonsense. "Well, we are nothing if not law abiding around here. I'll test the lights while you're gone."

"But don't start stringing them on the tree, okay? I want to help."

"You mean you want to give orders."

She grinned back at him and his heart flipped over. "Maybe," she admitted. "But you wouldn't want to end up with blank spaces and have to do it all over again, would you?"

He shot her a look that was part dare, part skepticism. "Who says I'd do it over?"

"It is Angela's first tree," she reminded him in that sweet, coaxing tone she used so effectively. "You want it to be perfect, don't you?"

He laughed. "So that's how it's going to be, is it? One teeny little mistake and you're going to accuse me of traumatizing the baby's entire perception of Christmas?"

He glanced down at Angela and saw that she'd fallen fast asleep amid her nest of pillows. "Look," he said triumphantly. "She's not even interested."

Jessie waved off the claim. "She won't sleep forever. Test the lights, but that's all, Lucas."

"Yes, ma'am."

When she'd gone, Luke tried to recall the last time he'd taken orders from anyone. Not once that he could think of since moving out of his father's house. More important, this was absolutely the only time he'd ever taken orders and actually enjoyed it.

Something had changed overnight, Jessie decided as she searched through her luggage for the festive red maternity sweater she'd bought for the holidays. She'd fallen in love with the scattered seed pearl trim around the neckline. Except for its roominess, it made a stylish ensemble with a pair of equally bright stirrup pants and dressy flats.

Suddenly she was overwhelmed by the Christmas spirit. It wasn't just the sight of that incredible tree. It was Luke's thoughtfulness in getting it for her. There was no mistaking that the tree and his shift in mood were his gifts to her.

She thought she'd seen something else in his eyes, as well, something she didn't dare examine too closely for fear she would confirm the attraction that had scared her away from White Pines.

Twenty minutes after she'd left him, she was back with a tray filled with mugs of steaming hot chocolate topped with marshmallows, and a plate of Christmas cookies she'd found in a tin, plus slices of her own homemade fruitcake. It made an odd sort of breakfast, but who cared? It fit the occasion. She also brought along the radio, which she immediately tuned to a station playing carols.

"Now?" Luke asked dryly, when she had everything set up to her satisfaction.

Jessie surveyed the ambience and nodded. "Ready. Did you check the lights?"

"All the strands are working," he confirmed. "More than we could possibly need even for this monster. I suspect half of them were used outside last year." He regarded her with a teasing glint in his eyes. "I assume you have a blueprint of some kind for their placement."

"Very funny."

He held out the first strand. "It's all yours."

Jessie's enthusiasm faltered slightly as her gaze traveled up the towering tree. "You have to do the first strand. I can't reach the top."

"I brought in a ladder."

She shot him a baleful look. "Never mind. Heights make me dizzy." So did Luke, but that was another story entirely. She was finding the powerful nature of her reactions to him increasingly worrisome.

"Are you sure you can trust me to do it right?" he teased.

"Of course," she said blithely. "I'll be directing you."

To his credit, he actually took direction fairly well. He seemed to lose patience only when she made him shift an entire strand one level of branches higher. "It'll be dark there, if you don't," she insisted.

"There are going to be a thousand lights on this tree at the rate we're going," he argued. "Nobody's even going to see the branches."

She turned her sweetest gaze on him. "The baby will like the lights."

The argument worked like a charm. Luke sighed and moved the strand.

"I'd better check the fuses before we turn this thing on," he complained. "It'll probably blow the power for miles around."

"Stop fussing. It's going to be spectacular. Let's do the ornaments next."

"Where did you intend to hang them? There's no space left."

She hid a grin at the grumbling. "Lucas, I could do this by myself."

He actually chuckled at that. "But you'd miss half the fun."

Jessie narrowed her gaze. "Which is?"

"Bossing me around."

"You have a point," she said agreeably. "But admit it, you're getting into the holiday spirit."

The teasing spark in his eyes turned suddenly serious. There was an unexpected warmth in his expression that made Jessie's pulse skitter wildly.

"I suppose I am," he said so quietly that she could practically hear the beating of her heart. "Can I tell you something?"

Jessie swallowed hard. "Anything."

"It's the first Christmas tree I've ever decorated."

She stared at him incredulously. "You're kidding."

He shook his head. "Mother always hired some decorator, who'd arrive with a new batch of the most stylish ornaments in the current holiday color scheme. We were never even allowed to be underfoot. By January second, it was all neatly cleared away, never to be duplicated."

"That's terrible," Jessie said. "I just assumed..."

"That we had some warm family tradition, like something out of a fairytale," he concluded. "You were there. You saw the fuss Mother made over choosing the design for the tree."

"I thought maybe it was something she'd started to do after you were all older and the family started doing more formal entertaining during the holidays."

"Nope. Not even when we came home from school with little handmade decorations. Those went on Consuela's tree. I think she still has them all. Mother paid a fortune for the perfect tree. She wasn't about to have the design marred by tacky ornaments made by her children."

Jessie's heart ached for the four boys who'd been deprived of the kind of tradition she'd always clung to. When she looked his way again, Luke's thoughtful gaze was on her as if he was waiting for her reaction to having one of her myths about his family shattered.

"Where are those decorations now?" she asked, clearly surprising him.

"In Consuela's suite, I suppose. Why?"

"Can you find them?"

He gave her an odd look. "Jessie, there's no need to get all sentimental about a bunch of construction paper and plaster of paris decorations."

"I want them on this tree," she insisted.

Luke shook his head at what he obviously considered a fanciful demand. "I'll take a look later."

"Promise?"

"I promise." He played along and solemnly crossed his heart. "What about you, Jessie? What was it like at your house?"

"Quiet," she said, thinking back to those days that had been a mix of happy traditions and inexplicable loneliness. "There were just the three of us. By the time I was adopted, my parents were already turning forty. There were no grandparents. I always thought how wonderful it would be if only there were aunts and uncles and cousins, but both of my parents had been only children."

"Is that why you were coming back to White Pines this year? Did you want to maintain the ties so your baby would eventually have the large family you'd missed?"

"That was part of it. That and wanting her to know she's an Adams. I don't have that sense of the past that you have. I suppose it can be a blessing and a curse—Erik certainly saw it that way—but I envy it more than I can tell you."

"Why didn't you ever search for your biological parents?"

She recalled how badly she'd once wanted to do exactly that. "I thought about it right after I learned I was adopted," she admitted. "But my parents were so distressed by the idea that I put it aside."

He paused in hanging the decorations and studied her from atop the ladder. "Is it still important to you?"

Jessie felt his gaze on her and looked up at him from her spot on the floor amid the rapidly emptying boxes. "I think it is," she said quietly. "It's as though there's a piece of me missing and I'll never be whole until I find it. It's funny. I thought Erik and your family could fill that space, but I was wrong. It's still there."

Luke climbed down from the ladder, then hunkered down in front of her and rested his hands on her knees. His gaze was even with hers and filled with compassion. "Then do it, Jessie. Find that missing part. I'll help in any way I can."

Something deep inside her blossomed under the warmth of his gaze. And for the first time she could ever recall, it seemed there was no empty place after all.

Chapter Seven

Though it tested her patience terribly, Jessie agreed
with Luke's idea that they not turn on the tree lights
until evening. The decision to wait left her brimming
with an inexplicable sense of anticipation, almost as
if she were a child again. She could recall year after
year when she'd huddled in her bed, pretending to
sleep, listening for the sound of reindeer on the roof,
the soft thud of Santa landing on the hearth after a
slide down the chimney. She wanted those kinds of
memories for her daughter, those and more.

She wanted Angela to grow up with memories of
Christmas Eves gathered around a piano singing carols, of midnight church services, and of the chaos of
Christmas morning with dozens of cousins and aunts
and uncles. She couldn't give her those things, but

Erik's family could. And as difficult as it might be at times to be around Luke without touching him, without openly loving him, she would see to it that the connection with the Adamses was never severed.

She glanced up to find Luke's gaze on her. She smiled, her eyes misty. "We'll make it sort of a Christmas Eve ceremony," she said, wondering at the magic that shimmered through her at the hint they were starting a tradition of their own. The memory of it was something she could hold tight, something no one could criticize or take away from her.

And yet, judging from the intent way Luke studied her, there must have been a note of sadness in her voice she hadn't realized was there.

"Are you sorry you're not spending Christmas Eve at my parents' house?" he asked.

There was an odd undercurrent to the question that Jessie couldn't interpret. Was he regretting not acting more aggressively to get her out of his hair? Or was the question exactly what it seemed? Was he worrying about her feelings?

"It's not the Christmas I was anticipating," she admitted, and saw the immediate and surprising flare of disappointment in his eyes. She hurried to reassure him. "It's better, Luke. No one could have done more to make this holiday special. You made sure I had a healthy baby. And how could I possibly regret the first Christmas with my daughter, wherever it is?"

Luke glanced at the baby she held cradled in her arms. Angela had just been fed and was already falling asleep again, her expression contented.

"She is what this season is all about, isn't she?" he said. "They say we don't always do so well with our own lives, but we can try harder to see that our children experience all of the magic of the holidays, that they get everything they deserve out of life."

His bleak tone puzzled her. "Luke, you sound as if your life is over and hasn't turned out the way you expected. That's crazy. There's still lots of time for you to fulfill all your dreams."

His inscrutable gaze met hers. Something deep in his eyes reached out and touched her. It was that odd sense of connection she'd felt so often in the past, as if their souls understood things they'd never spoken of.

"I'm not so sure about that," he said quietly. "I think maybe I missed out on the one thing that makes life worth living."

"Which is?" she asked, her voice oddly choked.

"Love."

Something in the way he was looking at her turned Jessie's blood hot. Her pulse thumped unsteadily. There was no mistaking the desire in his hooded eyes, the longing threading through his voice.

Nor was there any way to deny the stubborn set of his jaw that said he would never act on whatever feelings he might have for her. Fueled by guilt or conscience, he had declared her off limits.

Which was as it should be, Jessie told herself staunchly. Yet she couldn't explain the warring of regret and relief that his silent decision stirred in her. Stranded here with him, she didn't dare explore any of her feelings too closely, but she had been reminded sharply of all of them. Most especially she had remembered how a simple glance could warm her, how easily the soft caress of Luke's voice could send a tremor of pure bliss rippling through her.

At White Pines, with Erik alive, those responses had been forbidden. She had felt the deep sting of betrayal every time she hadn't been able to control her reaction to her husband's brother. Now it seemed the denials had gone for naught. Luke had reawakened her senses without even trying. He, thank goodness, appeared far more capable of pretending, though, that he hadn't. The charade of casual distance between them would be maintained to protect them both from making a terrible mistake.

"I think I'll put Angela down for a while," she said, practically dashing from the room that vibrated with unspoken longings.

Only after she had the baby safely tucked into her makeshift bed again, only after she was curled up in a blanket herself did she give free rein to the wild fantasies that Luke set off in her. Dangerous, forbidden fantasies. Fantasies that hadn't died, after all, not even after her attempt to put time and distance between herself and this complex man who'd found a spot in her heart with his unspoken compassion and strength of character.

"Oh, Lucas," she whispered miserably. "How could I have done it? How could I have gone and fallen in love with you?"

There was no point in denying that love was what she was feeling. She had fought it practically from the moment she'd first set eyes on him. She had run from it, leaving him and White Pines behind. But three nights ago, when Luke had been there for her, when he had safely delivered her baby and treated her with such tenderness and compassion, the powerful feelings had come back with a vengeance.

That didn't mean she couldn't go on denying them with every breath left in her. She owed that to Erik.

More than that, she knew as well as Luke obviously did, the kind of terrible price they would pay, the loss of respect from the rest of the family if he ever admitted what she was beginning to suspect...that he was in love with her as well.

Luke was slowly but surely going out of his mind. There wasn't a doubt about it. Another few days of the kind of torment that Jessie's presence was putting him through and he'd be round the bend. His body was so hard, so often, that he wondered why he hadn't exploded.

All it took was a whispered remark, an innocent glance, a casual caress and he reacted as if he were being seduced, which was clearly the farthest thing from Jessie's mind. There were times it seemed she could barely stand to be in the same room with him. She'd bolted so often, even a blind man would have gotten the message.

He couldn't understand why she, of all the women in the world, had this mesmerizing effect on him. Maybe guilt had made all of his senses sharper, he consoled himself. Maybe he wouldn't be up to speed and ready to rock and roll, if there weren't such an element of danger involved. He was practically hoarse from telling himself that Jessie was not available to him ever, and his body still wasn't listening!

It had been tough enough with Erik alive. His sense of honor had forbidden him from acting on his impulse to sweep Jessie into his arms and carry her off to his own ranch. Erik and Jessie had made a legal and religious commitment to love each other till eternity. Luke had witnessed their vows himself, had respected those vows, in deed, if not always in thought. He'd been tormented day in and day out by the longings he could control only by staying as far from Jessie as possible. With her right here in the home in which he'd envisioned her so often, his control was stretched beyond endurance. He was fighting temptation minute by minute. Each tiny victory was an agony.

A lesser man might not have fought so valiantly. After all, Erik's death had removed any legal barriers to Luke's pursuit of Jessie. But he knew in his heart it hadn't diminished the moral commitment the couple had made before God and their family and friends. Maybe if Luke told himself that often enough, he could keep his hands off her for a few more days.

But not if she impulsively threw her arms around his neck again, not if he felt the soft press of her breasts against his chest, or the tantalizing brush of her lips against his. A man could handle only so much temptation without succumbing—and hating himself for it forever after.

The safe thing to do, the smart, prudent thing would be to retrieve that blasted cellular phone from his truck and call his parents.

And he would do just that, he promised himself. He would do it first thing Christmas morning. Tomorrow, Jessie would be out of his home, out of his life. She would be back where she belonged—at White Pines—and back in her rightful role as Erik's widow, mother of Harlan and Mary's first grandchild.

Tonight, though, he would have Jessie and Angela to himself for their own private holiday celebration. Just thinking about sitting with Jessie in a darkened room, the only lights those on the twinkling tree they'd had such fun decorating, made his pulse race. They would share a glass of wine, listen to carols, then at midnight they would toast Christmas together.

And tomorrow he would let her—let both of them—go.

That was the plan. If he had thought it would help him stick to it, he would have written it down and posted it on the refrigerator. Instead, he knew he was going to have to draw on his increasingly tattered sense of honor. He stood in his office for a good fifteen minutes, his gaze fixed on Erik and Jessie's wedding picture just to remind himself of the stakes. He figured his resolve was about as solid as it possibly could be.

He tried to pretend that there was nothing special about the evening by choosing to wear one of his many plaid shirts, the colors muted by too many washings, and a comfortable, well-worn pair of jeans. Consuela would have ripped him to shreds for his choice. His mother would have declared herself disgraced. He considered it one small attempt to keep the atmosphere casual.

There were more. He set the kitchen table with everyday dishes and skirted the temptation of candles with careful deliberation. He would have used paper plates and plastic knives and forks if he'd had them just to make his point.

Still, there was no denying the festive atmosphere as he heated the cornish game hens with wild rice, fresh rolls and pecan pie that Consuela had left for his holiday meal. The wine was one of his best, carefully selected from the limited, but priceless, assortment in his wine cellar. The kitchen was filled with delicious aromas by the time Jessie put in an appearance.

She'd dressed in an emerald green sweater that had the look of softest cashmere. It hung loosely to just below her hips, suggesting hidden curves. Her slacks were a matching shade of wool. She'd brushed her coal black hair and left it to wave softly down her back.

"Something smells wonderful," she said peering into the oven. The movement sent her hair cascading over her shoulder. She shot him an astonished look. "Cornish game hens? Pecan pie?"

"Consuela," he confessed tightly as he fought the desire to run his fingers through her hair.

Her gaze narrowed speculatively. "She must have suspected you'd be having a special guest here for the holidays."

Was that jealousy in her voice? Luke wondered. Dear heaven, he hoped not. Jealousy might imply that his feelings were returned and he knew without any doubt that all it would take to weaken his resolve was a hint that Jessie felt as he did.

"Not suspected," he denied. "Hoped, maybe. Consuela is a hopeless romantic and my bachelor status is a constant source of dismay to her. She stays up nights watching old videos of Hepburn and Tracy, Fred Astaire and Ginger Rogers. I think she's worn out her tape of *An Affair to Remember.* She wakes me out of a sound sleep with her sniffling."

Jessie smiled. "A woman after my own heart. Maybe we should watch an old movie tonight. Does she have *It's A Wonderful Life* or *Miracle on 34th Street?*"

"I'm sure she does, but I refuse to watch them if you're going to start bawling."

"Can't stand to see a woman cry, huh?"

Certainly not this one woman in particular, he thought to himself. He would shift oceans, move continents if that's what it took to keep Jessie happy. His brother had broken her heart.

As soon as the disloyal thought formed, Luke banished it. Jessie had loved Erik. Their marriage had been solid. It wasn't for him to judge whether Erik's decisions had disappointed her. He dragged himself back to the present and caught Jessie studying him curiously.

"Nope, I never could stand to see a woman cry," he said, deliberately keeping his tone light. "I'm fresh out of hankies, too."

Jessie grinned. "No problem. I saw boxes of tissues stashed in the bathroom closet."

Luke heaved an exaggerated sigh of resignation. "I'll find the tapes right after dinner."

Dinner was sheer torture. Jessie found the candles Luke had avoided and lit them. The kitchen shimmered with candlelight and the glow from the fireplace. It was the kind of romantic lighting that turned a woman's complexion delectably soft and alluring, the kind of lighting that stirred the imagination. Luke's was working overtime. He could barely squeeze a bite of food past the lump lodged in his throat.

"You're awfully quiet," Jessie observed.

"Just enjoying the meal," he claimed.

She eyed his full plate skeptically. "Really?"

He was saved from stammering out some sort of explanation by the sound of whimpers from the bedroom. "Angela's awake," he announced unnecessarily and bolted before Jessie could even react.

With the baby safely tucked against his chest, it was easier somehow to keep his emotions in check. Right now he figured Angela was as critical to his survival as a bulletproof vest was to a cop working the violent streets.

"She's probably hungry," Jessie said when the two of them were settled back at the table.

The innocent observation had Luke's gaze suddenly riveted on Jessie's chest. So much for keeping his attention focused elsewhere.

"She's not making a fuss yet," he replied in a choked voice, clinging to the baby a trifle desperately. "Enjoy your dinner."

Jessie seemed about to protest, but finally nodded and picked up her fork. Luke kept his gaze firmly fixed on the baby.

"How are you doing, sweet pea? Ready for your very first Christmas? It's almost time for the big show, the lighting of the tree."

"It's amazing the effect you have on her," Jessie commented. "It must be your voice. It soothes her."

Luke grinned. "Can't tell you the number of women I've put to sleep by talking too much."

Blue eyes observed him steadily as if trying to assess whether he was only teasing or boasting. Apparently she decided he was joking. To his amazement, he could see a hint of satisfaction in her eyes.

"I doubt that," she countered dryly. "I suspect it's the kind of voice that keeps grown-up women very much awake."

"You included?" The words slipped out before he could stop them. His heart skidded to a standstill as he watched the color rise in her cheeks. Those telltale patches were answer enough. So he hadn't totally misread those occasional sparks of interest in her eyes. Nevertheless, a few sparks weren't enough to overcome a mountain of doubts.

Jessie seemed to struggle to find her voice. When she finally did, she said dryly, "Now that's the famous Luke Adams ego that's legendary around these parts."

"That's not an answer," he taunted, enjoying the deepening color in her cheeks.

"It's as close to one as you're likely to get," she taunted right back.

Luke chuckled. "Never mind. I already have my answer."

Jessie's gaze clashed with his, hers uncertain and very, very vulnerable. Luke finally relented. "You're immune to me. You've seen me at my worst."

"Bad enough to terrify the angels," she confirmed, her voice laced with unmistakable gratitude for the reprieve he'd granted.

She stood up with a brisk movement and reached for the baby, making her claim on the armor he'd clung to so desperately. "I'll feed her now," she said.

"You haven't had dessert," Luke protested, not relinquishing the baby. At this rate they'd be engaged in a tug-of-war over the child.

"We'll have it in front of the tree," Jessie said determinedly and held out her arms.

Reluctantly, he placed Angela in her mother's arms and watched them disappear down the hallway to the bedroom. Only when the door shut softly behind them did he breathe a heartfelt sigh of relief.

The reprieve, however, didn't last nearly long enough for him to regain his equilibrium. The clean-up kept him occupied briefly. Fixing coffee and pie to take into the living room took only moments longer.

In the living room, he plugged in the tree and turned on the radio, once again tuning it to a station playing carols. The room shimmered with a thousand twinkling colored lights. Luke was certain he had never seen a more beautiful tree, never felt so clearly the meaning of Christmas.

As he anticipated Jessie's return, he fingered the carved wooden figures in the crèche he'd placed beneath the tree, lingering over the baby Jesus. His thoughts were on another baby, one he wished with all of his jaded heart was his own.

He was standing, still and silent, when he sensed Jessie's approach. He heard her soft, indrawn breath. The faint scent of her perfume whispered through the air, something fresh and light and indescribably sexy.

"Oh, Luke, it's absolutely spectacular," she murmured. "The whole room feels as if it's alive with color."

He glanced down and saw reflected sparks of light shimmering in her eyes. Her lush mouth was curved in the sweetest smile he'd ever seen. Angela was nestled in her arms, spawning inevitable comparisons to the most finely drawn works of Madonna and child. In motherhood, even more than before, Jessie was both mysterious and beautiful, so very beautiful that it made his heart ache.

Nothing in heaven or hell could have prevented what happened next. Luke felt his control slipping, his resolve vanishing on a tide of desperate longing. He lowered his head slowly, pausing for the briefest of instants to gauge Jessie's reaction before gently touching his mouth to hers.

The kiss was like brushing up against fire, hot and dangerous and alluring. He lingered no longer than a heartbeat, but it was enough to send heat shimmering through him, to stir desire into a relentless, demanding need. The temptation to tarry longer, the need to savor, washed over him in great, huge, pulsing waves.

This one last time, though, the determination to cling to honor was powerful enough to save him, to save them both. He drew back reluctantly, examining

Jessie's dazed eyes and flushed cheeks for signs of horror or panic. He saw—or thought he saw—only a hunger that matched his own and, to his deep regret, the grit to resist, the impulse to run.

"Merry Christmas," he said softly before she could flee.

She hesitated, her eyes shadowed with worry. "Merry Christmas," she said finally, apparently accepting the truce he was offering in their emotional balancing act.

Luke hid a sigh of relief. She hadn't run yet and he had just the thing to see that she didn't. "I found Consuela's tapes. What'll it be?"

Jessie blinked away what might have been tears, then said, "*Miracle on 34th Street,* I think."

"Good choice," he said too exuberantly. He slid the tape into the VCR and flipped on the TV while Jessie settled herself and the baby on the sofa.

Luke warned himself to sit in a chair on the opposite side of the room, warned himself to keep distance between them. He actually took a step in that direction, before reversing and sinking onto the far side of the sofa.

Jessie shot him a startled look, then seemed to measure the space between them. Apparently it was enough to reassure her, because slowly, visibly she began to relax, her gaze fixed on the TV screen where the holiday classic was unfolding.

They could have been watching *Dr. Zhivago* for all Luke saw. He couldn't seem to drag his gaze or his thoughts away from Jessie. Each breath he drew was ragged with desire. Each moment that passed was sheer torment as his head struggled between right and wrong.

And yet, despite the agony of doing what he knew deep in his gut was right, he thought he had never been happier or more content. The night held promise tantalizingly out of reach, but it shimmered with possibilities just the same. A few stolen hours, he vowed. No more. He would soak up the scent of her, the sight of her so that every fiber of his being could hold the memory forever.

Her laughter, as light as a spring breeze, rippled over him leaving him aroused and aching. Tears spilled down her cheeks unchecked, luring his touch. His fingers trembled as he reached to wipe away the sentimental traces of dampness. At his touch, her gaze flew to his, startled... hopeful.

That hint of temptation in her eyes was warning enough. If Jessie was losing her resolve tonight, then being strong, being stoic was going to be up to him.

He withdrew his hand and thought it was the hardest thing he had ever done. Only one thing he could imagine would ever be harder—letting her go. And tomorrow, just a few brief hours from now, he would be put to the test.

Chapter Eight

Christmas morning dawned sunny and clear. The snow shimmered like diamonds scattered across white velvet. Sparkling icicles clung to the eaves. The world outside was like a wonderland, all of its flaws covered over with a blanket of purest white.

For once Jessie had apparently gotten up before Luke. She hadn't heard him stirring when she fed Angela at 6:00 a.m. Nor was there any sign of him in the kitchen when she went for a cup of coffee before showering and getting dressed. Usually starting the coffeepot was the first thing he did in the morning. Today it hadn't even been plugged in. Jessie checked to make sure the electric coffee machine was filled with freshly ground beans and water, then plugged it in and switched it on.

After tying the belt on her robe a little more securely, she sat down at the kitchen table to wait for the coffee to brew. Her thoughts promptly turned to the night before. Every single second of their holiday celebration was indelibly burned on her memory: the delicious dinner, the sentimental old movie, the shared laughter, the twinkling lights of the tree, the kiss.

Ah, yes, the kiss, she thought, smiling despite herself. She wasn't sure which one of them had been more shocked by its intensity. Even though Luke had initiated it, he had seemed almost as startled as she had been by the immediate flaring of heat and hunger it had set off. Though his mouth against hers had been gentle and coaxing, the kiss had been more passionately persuasive than an all-out seduction. Fire had leapt through her veins. Desire had flooded through her belly. If he had pursued his advantage, there was no telling how far things might have gone.

Well, they couldn't have gone too far, she reassured herself. She had just had a baby, after all. Still, there was no talking away the fact that she'd displayed the resistance of mush. And once again Luke had proven the kind of man he was, strong and honorable.

His restraint, as frustrating as it had been at the time, only deepened her respect for him. She added it to the list of all of his admirable traits and wished with all her heart that she had met him first, before Erik, before any possibility of a relationship had become so tangled with past history and old loyalties, so twisted with guilt and blame.

Almost as soon as she acknowledged the wish, guilt spread through her. How could she regret loving Erik? How could she possibly regret having Angela? Life had blessed her with a husband who had loved her with all his heart, no matter his other flaws. She had been doubly blessed with a daughter because of that love. What kind of selfish monster would wish any of that away?

"Dear God, what am I thinking?" she whispered on a ragged moan, burying her head on her arms.

There was only one answer. She had to find some way to get away from Luke, to put her tattered restraint back together. She had to get to White Pines before she made a terrible mistake, before the whole family was ripped apart again by what would amount to a rivalry for her affections.

Despite their occasional differences, she knew how deep the ties among Erik's family members ran. They would consider themselves the protectors of Erik's interests. Luke would be viewed as a traitor, a man with no respect for his brother's memory. They would hold her actions against him, blaming him alone for their love when the truth was that she was the one who was increasingly powerless to resist it. She wouldn't allow that to happen.

An image came to her then, an image of Luke returning from his pickup, his expression filled with guilt as he'd sworn he couldn't find his cellular phone. More than likely she'd been in denial that night, longing for something that could never be, or she would have known what that expression on his face had meant.

Anger, quite possibly misdirected, surged through her. It gave her the will to act, to do what she knew in her heart must be done. She stood and grabbed Luke's heavy jacket, poked her bare feet into boots several sizes too large, snatched up his thick gloves, and stomped outside.

She was promptly felled by the first drift of snow. She stepped off the porch and into heavy, damp snow up to her hips. She dragged herself forward by sheer will, determined to get to the truck, determined to discover if Luke had deliberately kept her stranded here.

Her progress could have been measured in inches. Her bare skin between the tops of the boots and the bottom of the coat was stinging from the cold. Still, she trudged on until she finally reached the pickup and tugged at the door. The lock was frozen shut.

Crying out in frustration, Jessie tried to unlock it by scraping at the ice, then covering the lock with her gloved hands in a futile attempt to melt the thin, but effective coating of ice. She tried blowing on it, hoping her breath would be warm enough to help. When that didn't work, she slammed her fist against it, hoping to crack it.

Again and again, she jiggled the handle, trying to pry the door open. Eventually, when she could barely feel her feet, when her whole body was shuddering violently from the cold, the lock gave and the door came free. She jumped inside and slammed the door, relieved to be out of the biting wind.

Remembering that Erik had always left the keys above the visor, no matter how she'd argued with him about it, she checked to see if Luke had done the same. No keys. She doubted Luke was any more security conscious than his brother had been. She checked under the floor mat, then felt beneath the front seat.

That's where she eventually found them, tucked away almost beyond her reach. Her fingers awkward from the gloves and the cold, she finally managed to turn on the engine. It might take forever for the truck to warm up, but she intended to spend as long as it took to thoroughly check the pickup for that cellular phone.

It didn't take nearly as long as she might have wished. To her astonishment and instantaneous fury, she found it on the first try, right in the glove compartment. Luke hadn't even bothered to lock it, though it was obvious to her that he had made a passing attempt to hide the phone under some papers. Clutching the phone in her hand, she sank back against the seat and simply stared at it.

"Luke," she whispered, "what were you thinking?"

She was so caught up in trying to explain her brother-in-law's uncharacteristic behavior that she didn't hear the crunching of ice or the muttered oaths until Luke was practically on top of her. Suddenly the passenger door was flung open—the damned lock didn't even stick under his assault—and Luke jumped into the seat beside her.

Jessie shot him an accusing look. His gaze went from her face to the cellular phone and back again. He muttered a harsh oath under his breath.

"It was here all along, wasn't it?" she asked in a lethal tone.

He didn't even have the decency to lie. He just nodded.

"Why, Luke?" Her voice broke as she asked. Unexpected tears gathered in her eyes, threatening to spill over. She felt betrayed somehow, though she couldn't have explained why. Maybe it was because she had expected so much more of Luke. The hurt cut deeper and promised worse scars than anything Erik had ever done.

Luke shoved his hand through his hair and stared off into the distance. He didn't speak for so long that Jessie thought he didn't intend to answer, but eventually he turned to face her, his expression haggard.

"I couldn't make the call," he said simply. "I just couldn't make it."

"Do you hate your family so much?" she demanded. "How could you let them worry about me? How could you leave them wondering if there'd been an accident? My heaven, they must be out of their minds by now."

He shot her a look filled with irony. "Do you really think that was what it was about?"

"What else?" she demanded, her voice rising until she didn't recognize it. "What else could have made you do something so cruel?"

Before she could even guess what he was about, he reached out and clutched the fabric of the coat that was several sizes too large for her. He dragged her roughly to him. This time when he claimed her mouth, there was nothing sweetly tentative about it. The kiss was bruising, demanding. It was the kiss of a desperate man, a man who had kept his emotions on a tight leash for far too long.

Jessie recognized the passionate claiming even before she felt the raging heat. Even as a protest formed in her head, exhilaration soared in her heart. Furious with herself for the weakness, she gave herself up to the magic of that kiss. His cheeks were stubbled, his skin cold, except where his mouth moved against hers. There, there was only the most tempting heat and she couldn't deny herself the pleasure of it.

As if he sensed that she wasn't fighting him, as if he realized that she was fully participating in this conflagration of sensation, Luke's rough touch became a softer caress. Demand gave way to the gentler persuasion. Out-of-control hunger turned to a far sweeter coaxing.

Jessie was captivated, her body aswirl with a riot of new feelings, more powerful than anything she'd ever felt with Erik. Not even her carefully cultivated battle against disloyalty could keep her from giving her all to this one devastating kiss.

This man, though, this timing... she couldn't help thinking how wrong it was, when she could think at all. A spark of pure magic scampered down her spine, chased by a shiver of doubt. She suspected they could thank bulky coats and thick gloves for checking their actions, more than they could credit either of them with good sense.

Eventually Luke cupped her face in his gloved hands. With his eyes closed and his forehead barely touching hers, he sighed heavily.

"Oh, Jessie, I never meant for this to happen," he said on a ragged, desperate note.

"But it has," she said, not sure whether that was cause for regret or joy. Only time would tell. "Now what?"

Luke released her and sank back against the passenger seat, his gaze fixed on the ceiling. "You take that phone and you go inside and call the folks. Daddy will find some way to pick you up before the day is out."

Somehow shocked at his matter-of-fact dismissal, Jessie stared at him. "You want me to go?" she whispered, devastated. "Now?"

"Especially now." His gaze determinedly evaded hers.

"But why? It's all out in the open at last. The way you feel. The way I feel. It was all there in that kiss. Don't tell me you can still deny it. There's no turning back now, Lucas. We have to deal with it."

If he was shocked by her feelings for him, he didn't show it. Instead, the look he turned on her was every bit as cold as the world outside that truck. "We are dealing with it. You're going and I'm staying. That's the way it has to be, the way it was meant to be."

Jessie shivered, chilled as much by his tone as the howling wind. "You can't mean that."

"I've never meant anything more," he insisted, his expression as steady and determined as she'd ever seen it. "Go to White Pines. It's where you belong."

A great, gnawing sensation started in the pit of Jessie's stomach. She sensed that if she did as he asked, if she left him here alone and went to be with his family, taking her place there as his brother's lonely, tragic widow, that would indeed be the end of it. Whatever might have been between them would die. Harlan, Mary, Jordan and Cody would be united in their opposition. The family and all of its complicated antagonisms and hurts would be like an insurmountable wall.

Well, she wouldn't have it. Maybe what she thought she felt for Luke was wrong. Maybe what he felt for her was some sort of terrible sin. Maybe they were both betraying Erik.

In a perfect world, her marriage would have fulfilled all of her dreams. It would have lasted a lifetime. And no man would ever have come along who was Erik's equal. She would have dutifully mourned until the end of time.

But her marriage hadn't worked. Erik had died. And Luke Adams was twice the man Erik had been. That wasn't her fault. It wasn't Erik's. In his own way, Erik had tried to make her happy. He had never realized that she couldn't be happy as long as he was so obviously miserable with the choices he alone had made for his life.

Nor, though, was the fault Luke's. Their feelings simply were there. He had done nothing to exploit them.

And she couldn't believe a benevolent God would have conspired to force her here to have her baby, if something more hadn't been meant to come of it. If there was one thing Jessie believed in with all her heart, it was fate. Surely God had brought them together not just to forgive, not just to rid themselves of guilt, but to love.

"I will only go to White Pines if you will come with me," she announced, her chin set stubbornly.

Luke stared at her, an expression of incredulity spreading across his handsome face. His mouth formed a tight line. Disbelief sparked in his eyes. "No way."

"Then Angela and I are staying."

"No way," he repeated more firmly, reaching for the cellular phone that had started them inevitably down this path and now lay forgotten in her lap.

Jessie's hand closed around it first and before Luke could react, she opened the car door and threw it with all her might. Landing silently, it disappeared slowly, inevitably in a soft drift of snow.

Luke's shocked gaze followed its path, then returned to her face. His jaw worked. Jessie waited for an explosion of outrage, but instead his lips curved into an unexpected smile. Amusement sparkled in his eyes. He seemed to be choking back laughter.

"The situation is not amusing, Lucas."

"It's not the situation, it's you. I can't believe you did that," he said at last.

She glared at him, not entirely sure what to make of this new mood. "Well, believe it."

"We might not find it till spring."

"So what?"

"You were the one who mentioned how cruel it was to leave my parents wondering and worrying about you."

Jessie's determination faltered ever so slightly. Apparently she was every bit as thoughtless as he was. "The phone lines are bound to be up soon. We'll call then."

He regarded her quizzically. "And if there's an emergency?"

"What kind of emergency?" She couldn't seem to keep a faint tremor out of her voice.

"The house burning down. The baby getting sick."

Jessie felt the color drain out of her face. "Oh, my God," she murmured, clambering out of the pickup. She tumbled into the snow, then struggled back to her feet. Before she could steady herself, Luke was beside her.

"You okay?"

"We have to get that phone."

He gave her an inscrutable look. "I'll get it. You go on inside. Despite the charming winter attire you appropriated from me, you're not really dressed for this weather."

She eyed him distrustfully. "You'll bring it inside?"

"Hey, I'm not the one who tried to bury it. I knew exactly where it was in case we really needed it."

She scowled at him. "Don't start trying to make yourself into a saint now, Lucas. It's too late."

He turned back and, to her astonishment, he winked at her. "It always was, darlin'."

Luke retrieved the cellular phone and barely resisted the urge to roll in the snow in an attempt to cool off his overheated body. The effect Jessie had on him was downright shameful. His blood pounded hotly through his veins just getting a glimpse of her. The kiss they had just shared could have set off a wildfire that would consume whole acres of prairie grass.

Damn, why had she been so willing? Why hadn't she smacked him, put him in his place, blistered him with scathing accusations? The instant he had hauled her into his arms, he'd half-expected the solid whack of her palm across his cheek. When it hadn't come, he'd dared to deepen the kiss, dared to pretend for just a heartbeat that he had a right to taste her, a right to feel those cool, silky lips heat beneath his, a right to feel her body shuddering with need against his.

The truth of it was, though, that he had no rights at all where Jessie was concerned. Even though she seemed to feel that that kiss had opened up a whole new world for the two of them, he knew better. He knew it had paved the way to hell, destroying good and noble intentions in its path.

He stuck the phone in his pocket and continued on to the barn, where he fed Chester and the horses. Chester nudged his hand away from his pocket, searching for his treat. Instead, there was only the phone.

"Sorry, old guy. I left the house in a hurry. I forgot your apple. I'll bring two when I come back later."

The old goat turned a sympathetic look on him, as if he understood the turmoil that had caused Luke to fail him.

"Good grief, even the animals are starting to pity me," he muttered in disgust and made his way back to the house, where he found Jessie singing happily as she worked at the stove.

The table had been set with the good china. Orange juice had been poured into crystal goblets. The good silver gleamed at each place. Luke eyed it all warily.

"It's awful fancy for breakfast, don't you think?"

"We're celebrating," she said airily.

He wasn't sure he liked the sound of that. It hinted that she wasn't letting go of the momentary craziness that had gripped the two of them in the pickup. "Celebrating what?"

She cast an innocent look in his direction. "Christmas, of course," she said sweetly.

"Oh."

She grinned. "Disappointed, Lucas?"

"Of course not." He glanced around a little desperately. "Where's Angela?"

"Sleeping."

"Are you sure? Maybe I should go check on her. She doesn't usually sleep this late."

Jessie actually laughed at that. "Surely a grown man doesn't have to rely on a three-day-old baby to protect him from me, does he?"

Luke felt color climb up the back of his neck and settle in his cheeks. "I just thought she ought to be here," he muttered. "It is her first Christmas morning."

"She'll be awake soon enough. Sit down. The biscuits are almost ready."

He stared at her incredulously as she bent over to open the oven door. The view that gave him of her fanny made him weak.

"When did you have time to bake biscuits?" he inquired, his voice all too husky.

"You were in that barn a long time," she said. She glanced over her shoulder. "Cooling off?"

Luke stared at her. What had happened to the sweet, virtuous woman who'd arrived here only a few days earlier? What did she know about her ability to drive him to distraction? *Get real, Lucas,* he told himself sternly. *She was as responsible for the heat of that kiss as you were.*

"Jessie," he warned, his voice low.

"Yes, Lucas?"

She sounded sweetly compliant. He didn't trust that tone for a second. "Don't get into a game, unless you understand the rules," he advised her.

"Who made up these rules? Some man, I suspect."

"Oh, I think they pretty much go back to Adam and Eve," he countered. He fixed his gaze on her until her cheeks turned pink. "I figure that gives 'em some credibility. People have been living by 'em for centuries now."

Jessie shook her head. Judging from her expression, she seemed to be feeling sorry for him.

"You are pitiful, Lucas," she said, confirming his guess.

He stared at her, a knot forming in his stomach. "Pitiful?"

"You don't know what to do about how you feel, so you start out hiding behind an itsy-bitsy baby and now you want to put God and the Bible between us."

"Right's right," he insisted stubbornly.

"And what was meant to be was meant to be," she countered, looking perfectly confident in making the claim.

Obviously she wasn't worried about the two of them being stricken dead by a bolt of lightning. Luke couldn't understand it. How could she be so calm, so sure of herself, when he'd never felt more off balance, more uncertain in all of his life?

"Whatever that means," he grumbled.

"It means, Lucas, that you might as well stop fighting so hard and accept the inevitable."

He studied her worriedly. "Which is?"

"Angela and I are in your life to stay."

He swallowed hard. "Well, of course you are," he said too heartily. "You're my sister-in-law. Angela's my niece."

Ignoring his comment, Jessie dished up scrambled eggs, bacon and golden biscuits. Only after she'd seated herself across from him did she meet his gaze.

"Give it up, Lucas. It's a battle you can't win."

Determination swept through him. "Try me," he said tightly.

To his annoyance, Jessie actually laughed at that. "Oh, Lucas, I intend to."

Chapter Nine

With Jessie's challenge ringing in his ears, Luke retreated to the barn. He figured it was the only safe place for him to be and still be within shouting distance of the house in case of a crisis. Inside, even in his office with the door shut, he couldn't escape Jessie's unrealistic expectations for their future. As brief as her presence had been, she had pervaded every room, leaving him with no place to hide from her or his unrelenting thoughts about her.

What she wanted from him, though, was impossible. How could they possibly have a relationship without bringing the wrath of the entire family she admired so much down on them? Couldn't she see that they were as doomed in their way as Romeo and Juliet had been? Or had she considered and then dismissed the problems? Could he possibly be that important to her?

He hunkered down on a bale of hay and distractedly tossed apple sections to Chester. The goat seemed to accept the unexpected largesse as his due. When Luke grew distracted and forgot to offer another chunk of apple, Chester butted him gently until he remembered. He scratched the goat behind his ears and wished that all relationships were this uncomplicated.

Dealing with goats and horses and cattle was a hell of a lot less troubling than dealing with a woman, Luke concluded when Chester finally tired of the game and wandered off. Food, attention, a little exercise, a few animal or human companions and their lives were happy. Women, to the contrary, sooner or later always developed expectations.

To avoid dealing with Jessie's fantasies, he considered saddling up one of the horses and riding off to check on the cattle. He manufactured a dozen excuses why such a trip was vital to the ranch's operations, even though he had a perfectly capable foreman in charge, a man who could probably account for every single head of longhorn cattle on the ranch without Luke's help.

Unfortunately, he could see through every excuse. He had no doubts at all that Jessie would be even quicker to see them for what they were: cowardly reasons to bolt from all the emotions he couldn't bear to face. While being someplace else—*anyplace else*—held a great deal of appeal at the moment, Luke wasn't a coward. Which meant, like it or not, staying and seeing this through.

Finally, tired of having only Chester and the horses for company when the most beautiful, if unavailable, woman in the world was inside, Luke heaved himself up and headed back to the house. Maybe Jessie had come to her senses while he was gone. Maybe his body had become resigned to celibacy.

And maybe pigs could fly, he thought despondently.

He found her sitting in front of the fireplace in the kitchen mending one of his shirts. As an inexplicable rage tore through him, he yanked the shirt out of her hands.

"What the hell are you doing?" he demanded.

Jessie didn't even blink at his behavior. "There was a whole basket of mending sitting in the laundry room waiting to be done," she said calmly as if that were explanation enough to offer a man who'd clearly lost his mind.

"Consuela's the housekeeper around here, not you."

"Is there some reason I shouldn't help her out?"

"It's her job," he insisted stubbornly.

Jessie merely shook her head, gave him that exasperating look that was filled with pity, and reached for another shirt. "It's my way of thanking her for all the meals she fixed before she left."

"She fixed them for me," Luke said, clinging to his stance despite the fact that even he could see he was being unreasonable. There was a quick and obvious remedy for what ailed him but he refused to pull Jessie into his arms, which was clearly where his body wanted her, where his long-denied hormones craved her to be.

One delicate eyebrow arched quizzically at his possessive claim on the meals Consuela had fixed. "Does that mean I'm no longer allowed to eat them?" Jessie inquired. "You planning to starve me into leaving?"

"Of course not," he snapped in frustration. "Just forget it. I'm going to my office."

"On Christmas?"

"If you can sew on Christmas, I can work."

"I'm not sure I see the connection," she commented mildly. She shrugged. "Whatever works for you."

Luke clenched his fists so tightly, his knuckles turned white. Why had he never noticed that Jessie was the most exasperating, the most infuriating woman on the face of the earth? She was so damned calm and . . . reasonable. He didn't miss the irony that he considered two such usually positive traits to be irritating.

To emphasize his displeasure, he plunked the cellular phone on the table in front of her. "Call my parents," he ordered tightly, then stalked away.

With any luck at all, Jessie would be tired by now of his attitude, he thought with only a faint hint of regret. After all, how long could a woman maintain this charade of complacency in the face of such galling behavior? She'd be packed and gone by the time he emerged from his office. His life could return to normal.

He glanced over his shoulder just as he headed through the doorway. She was humming to herself and, if he wasn't mistaken, there was a full-fledged smile on her face. He had the sinking realization that she wasn't going anywhere.

Jessie wasn't entirely sure why she was being so stubborn. One devastating, spine-tingling kiss hardly constituted a declaration of love.

Still, with every single bit of intuition she possessed, she believed that Luke was in love with her. That kiss was a symptom of stronger emotions. She was certain of it. She simply had to wait him out. Sooner or later, he would see that she wasn't afraid of the consequences if she stayed. He would see, in fact, that she welcomed them. Eventually he would realize that together they could even conquer all of the opposition they were likely to arouse.

The unexpected ringing of the cellular phone startled her so badly, she pricked her finger with the needle she'd been using to stitch buttons back onto Luke's shirts. Should she answer it? Or take it to Luke in his office? Of course, by the time she carried it through the house, whoever was calling would probably give up thanks to her indecisiveness.

It was guilt over her own failure to call Harlan and Mary that finally convinced her to answer on the fifth ring.

"Hello," she said tentatively.

"Who the hell is this?" Harlan Adams's unmistakable voice boomed over the line.

An odd mix of pleasure and dismay spread through her. "It's Jessie, Harlan. Merry Christmas!"

"Jessie?" he repeated incredulously. "You're okay. What the devil are you doing over at Lucas's? Why haven't you called? My God, woman, Mary's been out of her mind with worry."

Jessie decided that rather than responding to the questions and the barely disguised accusations Harlan had thrown out at her, she'd better go on the offensive immediately.

"I went into labor on the way to your house," she explained. "I was scared to death I'd deliver the baby in a snow drift. Luke's ranch was the only place nearby. You have a beautiful granddaughter, Harlan. I've named her Angela."

As she'd expected, the announcement took the wind out of his sails. "You've had the baby? A girl?"

"That's right."

"Mary," he called. "Mary! Get on the other line. Jessie's at Luke's and she's had the baby!"

Jessie heard the echoing sound of footsteps on White Pines's hardwood floors, then the clatter of a juggled, then dropped, phone. Finally, Mary's breathless voice came over the line. "You had the baby?"

"A girl," Jessie confirmed. "Angela. She is so beautiful, Mary. I can't wait for you to see her."

"But why are you at Luke's? Why not a hospital?"

"Angela was too impatient to get here. With the blizzard and everything, I figured this was my best bet."

"But the doctor did get there in time?" Mary asked worriedly.

Jessie hauled in a deep breath before blurting, "Actually, Luke delivered her. He was incredible. Calm as could be. You would have been so proud of him. I don't know what I would have done without him."

The explanation drew no response. Jessie could hear Mary crying. Eventually, Harlan spoke up.

"I don't get it, girl. That was three days ago. Why haven't you called before now?"

"The phone lines are down and Luke had misplaced the cellular phone. He hunted all over for it. It finally turned up this morning, buried under some papers." It was a stretch of the truth, but Jessie had no intention of filling them in on her own battle with Luke over this very phone.

"No wonder we couldn't reach him," Harlan grumbled. "That boy would lose his head if it weren't tacked onto his neck."

Jessie sighed. She'd never noticed that Luke was particularly absentminded, not about anything that mattered. The observation was just another of Harlan's inconsequential put-downs, uttered without thought to their accumulated cutting nature. She'd practically bitten her lower lip raw listening to him do the same thing to Erik. If she had thought it would help, she would have told him to stop, but she had known the order had to come from Erik.

"Well, it doesn't matter now," Harlan said. "Now that we know where to find you, I'll have my pilot pick you up in an hour. There's a landing strip not far from Luke's. He should be able to get you there."

"No," Jessie said at once.

"Beg pardon?" Harlan said, sounding shocked by her unexpected display of defiance.

"Jessie, darling, you must be anxious to be away from there," Mary protested. "We know how difficult it was for you to see Luke after what happened to Erik. Please, let Harlan send for you. We want you here with us and we can't wait to see the baby. You should be with family now."

"Luke is family," she reminded them.

"Yes, but...well, under the circumstances, you must be under a terrible strain there."

"No," Jessie insisted. She took a deep breath and prepared to manufacture an excuse that not even strong-willed Harlan Adams could debate. "The baby has no business being dragged around in weather like this, not for a few more days anyway. By then the roads will be clear and I can drive the rest of the way."

"Oh, dear," Mary promptly murmured. "She is okay, isn't she?"

"She's just fine, but she's a newborn and it's freezing outside. I'll feel better about bundling her up and taking her out in a few days, I'm sure."

"Well, of course, you must do what you think is best for the baby," Mary conceded eventually, but there was no mistaking her disappointment.

"Nonsense," Harlan said, heading down the single track his mind had chosen with dogged determination. "I'll send a doctor along in the plane to check her out. The baby ought to be seen by a professional as soon as possible, anyway. I'm sure Luke did his best, but he's not a physician. Don't worry about a thing, Jessica. I'll have Doc Winchell at Luke's before nightfall. Then you can all come back together. We'll have you here in time for the party Mary has planned. It'll be a celebration to end all celebrations."

"But, Harlan, it's Christmas," Jessie argued. "You can't expect the doctor or the pilot to disrupt their plans with their families to make a trip like that."

"Of course I can," Harlan countered with the assurance of a man used to having his commands obeyed. "You just be ready. I'll call back when they're on their way. Put Lucas on."

Defeated, Jessie sighed. "I'll see if I can find him."

She took the phone she deeply regretted answering down the hall to Luke's office. She tapped on the door, then opened it. He was leaning back in his leather chair, staring out the window. There was something so lonely, so lost in his expression that her heart ached. If only he would let her into his life, then neither of them would be alone again.

"Luke, your parents are on the line," she said and held out the phone.

He searched her face for a moment, his expression unreadable. Finally, he took the phone and spoke to his father.

"She's fine, Daddy. The baby's fine. I'm sure it's not the way Jessie would have preferred to deliver her baby, but there were no complications. She came through like a real trooper. She was back on her feet in no time. And the baby's a little angel."

He closed his eyes and rubbed his temples. "No, Daddy, I'm sure Jessie hasn't been overdoing it. She knows her own strength." His expression hardened and his gaze cut to Jessie again. "No, she didn't mention that you were sending Doc Winchell. I'm sure she'll be relieved. Right. We'll be expecting him.''

Most of Harlan's side of the conversation had been muffled, but Jessie heard him asking then if Luke intended to come to White Pines with her.

"No," Luke said brusquely. "I told Mother before that I have things to do here." His expression remained perfectly blank as he listened to whatever his father said next. Finally he said, "Yes, Merry Christmas to all of you, too. Give my best to Jordan and Cody."

He hung up the phone and turned back to the window. "Shouldn't you be packing?" he inquired quietly.

Tears welled up in Jessie's eyes. She hadn't expected him to be so stubborn. For some reason, she had thought when the time came, he would realize that he belonged at White Pines for the holidays every bit as much as she did. More so, in fact.

"I'm not leaving you here," she insisted.

He turned to confront her. "You don't have a choice. Harlan's taken it out of your hands. I told you that was exactly what would happen if you called him. It's for the best, anyway. It's time you were going."

"I didn't call. They called here." Jessie lost patience with the whole blasted macho clan of Adams men. "Oh, forget it. You can't bully me, any more than your father can. If I want to stay here, I'll stay here."

He regarded her evenly. "Even if I tell you that I want you to go?"

"Even then," she said, her chin tilted high.

"Why would you insist on staying someplace you aren't wanted?"

"Because I don't believe you don't want me here. I think you want me here too much," she retorted.

"You're dreaming, if you believe that," he said coldly.

Jessie's resolve almost wavered in the face of his stubborn, harsh refusal to admit his real feelings. "I guess that's the difference between us, then. I believe in you. I believe in *us*. You don't."

"That's a significant difference, wouldn't you say?"

"It's only significant if you want it to be."

"I do."

A tear spilled over and tracked down her cheek. "Damn you, Luke Adams."

"You're too late, Jessie," he told her grimly. "I was damned a long time ago."

For all of her natural optimism, for all of her faith in what a future for the two of them could hold, Jessie couldn't stand up to that kind of bleak resignation.

"Angela and I will be gone before you know it," she said, fighting to hold back her tears as she finally admitted that she was defeated.

In the doorway she paused and looked back. "One of these days you're going to regret forcing us out of your life, Luke. You're going to wake up and discover that you've turned into a bitter, lonely old man."

That said, she straightened her spine and walked away from the man she'd come to love with all her heart.

* * *

Regrets? Luke was filled with them. They were chasing through his brain like pinballs bouncing erratically from one bumper to the next.

Was he doing the right thing? Of course, he was, he told himself firmly. He had to let Jessie go. He had to let her walk out of his life, taking the baby who'd stolen a little piece of his jaded heart with her. They weren't his to claim. They were Erik's and they were going home, where they belonged. They were going to a place where he no longer fit in.

He would have stayed right where he was, hidden away in his office, but Jessie was apparently determined to make him pay for forcing her out of his life. She appeared in the doorway of his office, bundled up, her long hair tucked into a knit cap, her cheeks rosy, either from anger or from a trek outdoors. He suspected the former.

"We're leaving," she announced unnecessarily.

Luke had seen Doc Winchell arrive in a fancy four-wheel-drive car a half hour earlier cutting a path through the fresh snow. He'd been expecting to see it driving away any minute now heading back to the airport. He'd been listening for the sound of the back-door slamming shut behind them, then the roar of the car's engine. The silence had taunted him. Now, though, it seemed they were finally ready to go, and he was going to be forced to endure another goodbye.

"Have a safe trip," he said, refusing to meet her condemning gaze.

"Aren't you going to come and say goodbye to Angela?"

"No," he said curtly and felt his heart break.

"Lucas, please."

She didn't know what she was asking, that had to be it, he decided as he finally got to his feet and followed her into the kitchen.

Doc Winchell, who'd been the family physician ever since Luke could recall, beamed at him. "Lucas, you did a fine job bringing this little one into the world. Couldn't have done better myself. We'll get her weighed and checked out from head to toe tomorrow, but she looks perfectly healthy to me."

Luke kept his gaze deliberately averted from the bundled-up baby. "She really is okay, then?"

"Perfect," the doctor confirmed.

"Being out in this weather won't hurt her?"

"The truck's heater works. She's wrapped up warmly. She'll be fine."

"What about flying?"

"It shouldn't be a problem and I'll be right there to keep an eye on her."

Luke nodded, his hands shoved in his pockets to keep from reaching out to hold the baby one last time. "Take good care of her, Doc. She's my first delivery." He grinned despite himself. "Hopefully, my last, too. I don't think I ever want to know that kind of fear again."

As if she sensed that Angela was his Achilles' heel, Jessie plucked the baby up and practically shoved her into Luke's arms. He had to accept her or allow her to tumble to the floor. One look into those trusting blue eyes and he felt his resolve weaken.

"Say goodbye, Angela," Jessie murmured beside him. "Uncle Luke isn't coming with us."

As if she understood her mother, Angela's face scrunched up. Her tiny lower lip trembled. Huge tears welled up in her eyes.

Luke rocked her gently. "Hey, little one, no tears, okay? Your Uncle Luke will always have a very special spot in his heart, just for you. You ever need anything, anything at all, you come to me, okay, sweet pea?"

As always, the sound of his voice soothed her. She cooed at him. His effect on her gave him a disconcerting sense of satisfaction. He felt as if his sorry existence meant something to somebody.

Jessie seemed to guess what he was feeling. Her gaze, filled with understanding and a kind of raw agony, was fixed on his face. Luke couldn't bear looking into her eyes. She knew too well why he was pushing them away. He looked back at Angela's precious little face instead.

"Goodbye, sweet pea. You take good care of your mommy, okay?"

He held the baby out until Jessie finally had no choice but to claim her.

"Goodbye, Lucas," she said, her voice laced with all the regret he was feeling. "I will never, ever forget what you did for us."

He wanted to tell her it was nothing, but he couldn't seem to force the words past the lump lodged in his throat. He just nodded.

Jessie reached up then and touched her hand to his cheek, silently commanding him to look at her. When he did, she said softly, "If you ever, *ever* change your mind, I'll be waiting."

"Don't wait too long," he warned. "Don't waste your life waiting for something that can never be."

For an instant he thought she was going to protest, but finally she sighed deeply and turned away. She walked out the kitchen door and never looked back.

It was just as well, Luke thought as he watched her. He would have hated like hell for her to see that he was crying.

Chapter Ten

The commotion caused by their arrival at White Pines was almost more than Jessie could bear, given her already-confused and deeply hurt state of mind.

Harlan gave Doc Winchell the third degree about the baby's health. Mary claimed Angela the minute Jessie set foot across the threshold. Jordan and Cody studied the new baby with fascination, offering observations on which family members she most resembled. A handful of strangers, visiting for the holiday, chimed in.

They had almost nothing beyond the courtesies to say to Jessie, and not one of them asked about Luke. It was hardly surprising, she concluded, that he had refused to set foot in the house at White Pines.

As she stood apart and watched them, Jessie couldn't help wondering why she'd once wanted so desperately to be a part of this family. It suddenly seemed to her that she'd mistaken chaos and boisterous outbursts for love.

Of course, back then she'd had Erik as a buffer. He'd seen to it that she was never left out of the conversation. He'd insisted that she be treated with respect. She had basked in his attention and barely noticed anyone else.

Except Luke.

Thinking of him now, all alone again on his ranch, she regretted more than ever leaving him, despite his cantankerous behavior. She should have risen above it. She should have listened to her heart.

Suddenly she couldn't stand all the fussing for another instant. Reaching for Angela, she startled them all by announcing that the baby was tired from the trip and needed to be put down for a nap. To her astonishment, no one argued. She would have to remember that tone of voice for the next time someone in the family tried to steamroll over her.

"I found an old crib in the attic," Mary said at once. "I had Jordan set it up in your old suite. As soon as the rest of the roads have cleared and it's safer to drive, we'll go into town for baby clothes and new sheets and blankets. In the meantime, I've had Maritza wash a few things I saved from when the boys were babies."

Jessie fought a grin as she tried to imagine sexy, irrepressible Cody, the tall, self-assured Jordan or Luke ever being as tiny as Angela was now. "Thank you," she said. "I'm sure we'll be fine."

Cody separated himself from the others as she started up the stairs. "How is Luke?" he asked, walking along with her. Lines of worry were etched in his brow that she was sure hadn't been there mere months before. He was only twenty-seven, but he seemed older, wearier than he had when she'd left.

"Stubborn as a mule," she said. "Lonely."

"Why didn't he come with you?"

Jessie met Cody's concerned gaze and gave him the only part of the real answer she could. The rest was private, just between her and Luke. She couldn't say he was staying away because of her. "Because he blames himself for Erik's death, and he thinks the rest of you do, too."

Cody couldn't have looked more shocked if she'd announced that Luke was locked away at home with a harem.

"But that's crazy," he blurted at once. "We all know what happened was an accident. Nobody blames Luke. Hell, if anybody was at fault it was Daddy. He's the one who backed Erik into a corner and made him try to be something he wasn't. Any one of us could have taken a spill on that tractor. Accidents happen all the time on a ranch."

Jessie couldn't have agreed with him more, but she was startled that Cody recognized the truth. Of all of them, he had always seemed to be the least introspective. Cody seemed imperturbable, the one most inclined to roll with the punches. She'd always thought he accepted things at face value, including Harlan's own view of himself as omnipotent. Obviously she'd fallen into the trap of viewing him merely as the baby in the family. The truth was he'd grown into a caring, thoughtful man.

"That's what I tried to tell Luke, but the accident didn't happen here. It happened on his land. He seems to think he should have prevented it somehow." She looked into Cody's worried eyes. "Talk to him. Maybe you can get him to see reason. I couldn't."

Cody looked doubtful. "Jessie, if you couldn't reach him, I don't see how I can. You were always able to communicate with him, even when the rest of us were ready to give up in frustration."

Jessie sighed. "Well, not this time."

At the doorway to the suite she had shared with Erik she paused. Cody leaned down and brushed a light kiss across her cheek. "I'm glad you're back, Jessie. We've missed you around here. I think the last ounce of serenity around this place vanished the day you left."

She was startled by the sweet assessment of her importance to this household where she'd always felt like an interloper. "Thanks, Cody. Saying that is the nicest gift anyone could have given me."

He grinned. "Don't say that until you've opened those packages downstairs. Something tells me everyone's gone overboard in anticipation of your return and the arrival of the baby." He winked at her. "One thing this family is very good at is bribery."

"Bribery?"

"So you'll stay, of course. You don't think Daddy will be one bit happy about his first grandbaby growing up halfway across the state. He's going to want to supervise everything from cradle to college. Hell, he'll probably try to handpick her husband for her. Just be sure he doesn't make her part of some business deal."

Before Jessie could react to that, Cody was already thundering down the stairs again.

"Cody, for heaven's sakes, remember where the dickens you are," Harlan bellowed from somewhere downstairs.

"I'm just in a hurry to get another slice of Maritza's pie," Cody shouted back, unrepentant.

"No more pie until dinner," Mary called out. "There won't be a bit left for the rest of us."

"Mother, Maritza's been baking for a month," Cody retorted. "There must be enough pies in the kitchen to feed half of Texas. You've only invited a quarter of the state at last count. One slice won't be missed."

Jessie stood for a moment longer, listening to the once-familiar bickering and decided that this, too, was what it meant to be part of a family. Somehow, though, with neither Erik nor Luke here the atmosphere had lost something vital—its warmth.

Feeling thoughtful and a little lonely, she opened the door to her suite, took a deep breath . . . and walked back into her past.

The house was empty. Luke found himself wandering from room to room, hating the oppressive silence, hating the sense of loneliness that he'd never noticed before. He'd always been a self-contained man. Hell, any cowboy worth his salt could spend

days on end in the middle of nowhere, content with his
own thoughts.

Suddenly he didn't like his own company all that
much. In a few short days, he'd grown used to Jessie
invading his space at unexpected moments. He'd come
to look forward to his own private time with Angela,
their one-sided conversations, her sober, trusting gaze.

He stood at the doorway to his own bedroom and
tried to force himself to cross the threshold. For some
idiotic reason, he felt as if he were trespassing on Jessie's private space, rather than reclaiming his own.

She'd left the room spotless, far neater than it had
been when she'd arrived. The bed had been made up
with fresh sheets. He knew because he'd heard the
washing machine and dryer running and investigated.
He'd found sheets and towels in the dryer, a load of his
clothes in the washer.

He sighed. He almost wished she had left the old
sheets on. Perhaps then, when he finally crawled back
into that lonely bed of his, he might have been surrounded by her scent. Now, he knew, it would smell
only of impersonal laundry detergent and the too-
sweet fabric softener.

As he stood there he caught the glint of something
gold on the nightstand beside the bed. The last rays of
sunshine spilled through the window and made the
metal gleam, beckoning him. Instinctively he knew
whatever it was, it wasn't his. Puzzled, he crossed the
room to see what Jessie had left behind.

Even before he reached the nightstand, he realized
what it was: a ring. Her wedding ring. His heart
skipped a beat at the sight of it. He picked up the

simple gold band and let it rest in the palm of his hand. Even though he knew what it said, he read the engraved message inside: Erik and Jessica—For Eternity.

What had she been thinking? he wondered. She must have taken it off when she was cleaning and simply forgotten it, he decided because he wasn't sure he wanted to consider any other implications. He didn't want to believe that she'd been deliberately making a statement, leaving him an unmistakable message that would force him to act or forever damn himself for his inaction.

Eventually he pocketed the ring and returned to the kitchen and poured himself a cup of coffee. He put the ring on the table in front of him as he sipped the rank brew that had been left since morning.

What the devil was he supposed to do now? He could mail it to her at White Pines. Unfortunately, the arrival of her wedding ring in the mail might stir up a hornet's nest, if anyone in the family happened to notice. Heaven knew what interpretation they might place on her leaving it behind. He hadn't even figured out his own interpretation of its significance.

If an outsider saw him, he'd think Luke had lost his mind, Luke acknowledged dryly. He was studying that tiny ring as if it were a poisonous snake, coiled to strike. The truth was, though, that the ring's presence in his bedroom was every bit as dangerous as any rattler he'd ever encountered.

"Seems to me like there are two choices here," he finally muttered, his gaze fixed on the gold band. "Send it off and quit worrying about it or call her up and ask what the devil she had in mind. Sitting here trying to make sense of it isn't accomplishing a blessed thing."

It was also leading him to talk to himself, he noted ruefully.

He carried the coffee and the ring into his office, where he'd left the cellular phone. He sat behind his desk for several minutes, trying to figure out what he could say that wouldn't make him look like an idiot. Finally he just dialed the damn number, taking a chance that Jessie would be in her old suite and that it would still have the private line Erik had had installed. She answered on the first ring.

"Jessie?"

There was the faintest hesitation before she asked, "Lucas? Is that you?"

Something inside him suddenly felt whole again at the sound of her voice. It was a sensation that probably should have worried him more than it did. "Yeah, it's me," he confirmed. "How was your flight? Any problems?"

"No, everything went smoothly. Angela never even woke up."

"That's good. I imagine everyone there made quite a fuss when they saw her."

"That's an understatement," she said. "According to Cody, your father will probably want to plan out her entire life, up to and including her choice of a husband."

Luke found himself laughing at the accuracy of his youngest brother's assessment. "Listen to him. He has the old man pegged."

That said, he suddenly fell silent.

"Luke?"

"Yes."

"Was that all you wanted, to see if we'd arrived okay?"

He sighed. "No." Without quite realizing that he'd reached a decision on his approach, he blurted out, "Actually, I wanted to let you know that you'd forgotten your wedding ring. You must have taken it off when you were cleaning or something."

"I didn't forget it," she said, a note of determination in her voice.

Her response left him stymied. "Oh," he said and then fell silent again, struggling with the possibilities, fighting a flare of hope he had no business at all feeling. Finally he asked, "Why, Jessie?"

"Think about it, Lucas," she said softly and he could almost see her smiling. "You're a bright man. You'll figure it out."

"Jessie..."

"Goodbye, Luke. Merry Christmas."

She hung up before he could get in another word. He sat staring stupidly at the phone in his hand. He closed his eyes and wished with all his heart that he'd gone to the Caribbean for the holidays. Or maybe taken a trip to Australia. Or even the South Pole.

Then he remembered that Jessie would have found the house empty when she'd gone into labor on the highway. Who knew what might have happened then. He couldn't regret having been here for her. No matter how much pain his feelings for her caused him in the future, he couldn't regret these few days they'd had.

He just had to figure out how to make them last a lifetime.

Jessie gently placed the telephone receiver back in its cradle and turned to the wide-awake baby on the bed beside her.

"That was your Uncle Luke," she whispered, unable to keep a grin from spreading across her face. Just hearing his voice made her pulse do unexpected somersaults.

Angela understood. Jessie was absolutely certain of it. She waved her little fist in the air approvingly.

"How long do you figure it's going to take him to show up here?" Jessie wondered aloud.

She was far more confident now that he would turn up than she had been when she'd ridden away from his ranch with Doc Winchell. Leaving her own car there had been her ace in the hole. If Luke didn't make the trip to White Pines, after all, she knew she could always go back to get her car and have one last chance at making him see what they could have together.

She rolled onto her back, only to have her wedding picture catch her eye. It was still sitting on the dresser, just as it had while she and Erik had lived in this suite.

"You understand, don't you?" she whispered with certainty. "You've forgiven Luke and me for falling in love and that's all that really matters."

A soft tap on her door quieted her. "Jessie?" Mary called softly. "We'll be serving dinner in half an hour."

"I'll be right down," she promised.

"Bring the baby. I've found a carrier for her. I'll leave it outside the door."

"Thanks, Mary."

Jessie listened as her mother-in-law's footsteps faded, then she glanced down at her daughter. "Showtime, angel. It's time to go and dazzle your family."

The baby waved her arms energetically, an indication that she was more than ready for anything the Adams clan had in mind for her—now or in the future. Jessie wished she could say the same.

She had no sooner reached the bottom step, when Jordan appeared to take the carrier from her. At thirty, he was a successful businessman, one of the few to weather the Texas oil crisis and come out ahead. He was considered one of the state's most eligible catches, but he had remained amazingly immune to any of the women who chased after him.

"You look lovely, Jessie." He glanced down into the carrier, his expression faintly nervous as if he weren't too sure what to do with a baby. He seemed worried she might be breakable. "Everyone's anxious to see the newest addition to the family."

Jessie hesitated. "By everyone, I assume you mean that this isn't just a family celebration tonight."

Jordan's mouth quirked in a grin that reminded her so much of Luke, she felt her heart stop.

"Nope. The usual cast of thousands," he said. He leaned down and whispered, "Stick close to me and I'll protect you from the multitudes."

"And what about your own date?" she whispered right back. "I know perfectly well you must have one here. I've never seen you without a beautiful woman on your arm."

A flicker of something that might have been sadness darkened his eyes for just an instant, before his ready smile settled firmly back in place.

"I decided even I deserved a night off," he replied.

"Tired of small talk?" Jessie asked.

"Tired of all of it," he admitted. When Jessie would have questioned him further about whether this indicated an end to his days as Houston's most available playboy, he prevented it by taking her arm and propelling her into a room already crowded with guests.

"Behold the heir apparent," he announced, holding the baby carrier aloft as everyone applauded. That said, he seemed only too anxious to turn the baby over to the first person who asked to hold her. He wandered off without a second glance, his duty done.

For the second time since her arrival at White Pines, Jessie was gently shunted aside by people anxious to get a glimpse of the newborn. She heard the story of her being stranded at Luke's ranch told over and over. She heard her own bravery magnified time and again.

What she never heard, though, was any mention of Luke's incredible role in any of it. Just when she was prepared to climb halfway up the stairs and demand that everyone listen to her version of the events, Harlan folded a strong arm around her shoulders and called for silence.

"A toast," he announced. "Everybody have some champagne?"

Glasses were lifted into the air all around them.

"To Jessie and Angela," he said. "Welcome home."

The toast echoed around the room, as heartfelt from strangers as it was from the family. Even so, the welcome left Jessie feeling oddly empty. White Pines no longer felt like home. What saddened her more was that she wasn't sure whether it was the loss of Erik or the absence of Luke that made her feel that way.

When the cheers had died down, Harlan announced that the buffet supper was ready. The guests moved swiftly into the huge dining room to claim their plates and a sampling of the food that Jessie knew Maritza and the rest of the staff had been preparing for weeks now. She recalled from past years how bountiful and diverse the spread would be, but her own appetite failed her.

She surveyed the room until she finally spotted Cody holding her daughter and went to join them.

"I'll take her," she offered. "Go on and have your dinner."

Cody grinned. "I don't mind. I'm practicing my technique. I figure if I can charm 'em when they're this little, I'll have no problems with the grown-up ladies."

"Well, Angela's certainly fascinated," Jessie agreed as she observed her daughter's fist tangled in Cody's moustache. The baby tugged enthusiastically and Cody winced, but he didn't give her up. He simply disengaged her fingers as he chattered utter nonsense to her. Like Luke, he seemed totally natural and unselfconscious with the infant in his arms.

"You might have to work on your conversational skills," Jessie teased, after listening to him.

"You're not the first woman to tell me that," he admitted with a wicked grin that probably silenced most women on the spot, anyway. Jessie was immune to it, but she found herself amused by his inability to curb the tendency to flirt with any female in sight.

"I guess it's what comes from spending most of my days with a herd of cows," he added. "They're not too demanding."

"And what about Melissa?" she inquired, referring to the young woman who'd been head over heels in love with Cody practically since the cradle. "Is she too demanding?"

Cody's eyes lit up at the mention of the woman everyone assumed he would one day marry, if he ever managed to settle down at all. "Melissa hangs on my every word," he said confidently.

The touch of arrogance might have annoyed some people, but Jessie knew that Cody's ego wasn't his problem. The young man was simply a textbook case of a man who was commitment phobic. Melissa had contributed to the problem by wearing her heart on her sleeve for so long. Cody tended to take her for granted, certain she would be waiting whenever he got around to asking her to marry him.

One day, though, either Melissa or some other woman was going to turn Cody inside out. Jessie smiled as she envisioned the havoc that would stir.

"What are you grinning about?" Cody asked.

"Just imagining how hard your fall is going to be when it comes. Yours and Jordan's."

"Won't be any worse than Erik's," he teased. "Or Luke's," he added, shooting her a sly look.

Jessie swallowed hard. "Luke's?" she said, feigning confusion.

"I'm not blind, Jessie. Neither is anyone else around here, for that matter. Why do you think they were so appalled when they realized where you were when you had the baby? Luke never did have much of a poker face."

She was stunned. "What are you saying?"

"That my big brother is crazy in love with you. Always has been. Luke may be the strong, silent type, but he's transparent as can be where you're concerned."

Even as her heart leapt with joy at his confirmation of her own gut-deep assessment of Luke's feelings, Jessie denied Cody's claim. "You're wrong," she insisted.

Cody shook his head, clearly amused by her protest. "I'm not wrong. Why do you think he's not here?"

"I explained that earlier. It's because he's feeling guilty about Erik's death."

"He's feeling guilty, all right, but it's not because of Erik's death. At least, that's only part of it," he told her emphatically. "Luke's all twisted up inside because he's in love with Erik's widow."

Jessie practically snatched Angela out of Cody's arms. When she would have run from the room, when she would have hidden from Cody's words, he stopped her with a touch.

"Please, Jessie, I didn't mean to upset you. I, for one, think it would be terrific if you and Luke got together. Erik's gone. We can't wish him back. And if you and Luke can find some kind of happiness together, then I say go for it. Jordan agrees with me. He seems to be looking for happy endings these days. Don't say I told you but I think the confirmed bachelor is getting restless," he confided. "He needs you and Luke to set an example for him."

Once more, Cody had startled her, not just with his assessment of the undercurrents that she thought had been so well hidden in the past, but with his blessing.

"I don't know what the future holds," she said quietly, the words as close to an admission about her own feelings as she could make. "But I will always be grateful to you for speaking to me so honestly."

Cody draped an arm around her shoulders and squeezed. "Hey, Luke might be stubborn as a mule, but he is my big brother. I want him to be happy. As for you, the whole family lucked out when Erik found you. We want to keep you. And there's Angela to think of," he said, touching a finger gently to the baby's cheek. "She deserves a daddy and I think Luke would make a damned fine one."

Only after he had walked away did Jessie whisper, "So do I, Cody. So do I."

Chapter Eleven

Luke could see only one way to push Jessie out of his life once and for all. If she had chosen Erik because she wanted a family to call her own, if she clung to him now for the same reason, then he would give her one. Not his, but her own. Her biological family.

He'd been awake half the night formulating his plan. First thing in the morning on the day after Christmas, he was on the phone to a private investigator he'd used once when he'd suspected a neighbor of doing a little cattle rustling from his herd. He supposed finding a long-lost family couldn't be much trickier than tracing missing cattle.

"Her adoptive family's name was Garnett," Luke told James Hill, dredging up the surname from his memory of the first time Jessie had been introduced to the family, practically on the eve of the wedding. Erik hadn't risked exposing her to too many of his father's tantrums or too many of his mother's interrogations. It was probably one of his brother's wisest decisions. Jessie might have fled, if she'd realized exactly what she was getting into. The surface charm of the family disintegrated under closer inspection.

"What else can you tell me about her?" Hill asked.

"What do you mean?"

"Where was she born? Where did she grow up? Her birth date? Anything like that?"

Luke listened to the list and saw his scheme going up in flames. For the first time he realized how very little he actually knew about Jessie. He'd fallen in love with the woman she was now. It had never crossed his mind that he might want to be acquainted with the child she had been or the lonely teenager who'd longed to discover her real family.

"I don't know," he confessed finally.

"You'll have to find out something or it'll be a waste of my time and your money," the private investigator informed him. "With what you're giving me, I can't even narrow the search down to Texas."

Luke sighed. "I appreciate the honesty. I'll see what I can find out and call you back. Thanks, Jim."

"No problem. If I don't talk to you before, have a Happy New Year, Luke."

"Same to you," he said, but his mind was already far away, grappling with various ideas for getting the information he needed about Jessie without her finding out what he was up to. He didn't want her disappointed if he failed to find answers for her.

To his deep regret, he could see right off that there was only one way. He would have to follow her to White Pines. The only way he could ask his questions was face-to-face, dropping them into the conversation one at a time over several days so she wouldn't add them up and suspect his plan. If the thought of seeing her again made his palms sweat and his heart race, he refused to admit that his reaction to the prospect of seeing her had anything at all to do with his decision to go. The trip was an expediency, nothing more.

For the second time that morning, Luke made a call he'd never in a million years anticipated making.

"Hey, Daddy, it's Luke."

"Hey, son, how are you?" Harlan asked as matter-of-factly as if Luke initiated calls to White Pines all the time. If he was startled by Luke's call, he hid it well.

"I'm fine."

"What's up?"

He drew in a deep breath and finally forced himself to ask, "Can you send the plane for me? I'm coming home."

Dead silence greeted the announcement, and for the space of a heartbeat Luke thought he'd made a terrible mistake in calling, rather than just showing up. It had been less than twenty-four hours since he'd flatly declared he wouldn't be coming to White Pines. If his father started one of his typical, if somewhat justifiable, cross-examinations, Luke didn't have any answers he was willing to share. He waited, unconsciously holding his breath, to see how his father would handle this latest development in their uneasy relationship.

"I'll have the plane there in an hour," his father said finally. It was as though he'd struggled with himself and decided to give his son a break for once.

Luke heaved a sigh of relief. "Thanks."

"No problem," Harlan said. He paused, then added, "But if you go and change your mind on me, though, I'm warning you that you'll pay for the fuel."

Luke laughed at the predictable threat, relieved by it. Obviously Harlan hadn't mellowed that much. "That's what I love about you, Daddy. You never allow sentiment to cloud your thinking about the bottom line."

By the time Jessie got downstairs for breakfast on the morning after Christmas, only Mary remained at the table. She looked as stylish and perfectly coiffed as she had the night before, despite the fact she couldn't have had more than a few hours sleep.

Last night, surrounded by family and old friends, by the famous and the powerful, she had been in her element. She was equally at ease at the head of the table with only her daughter-in-law to impress. Jessie found that polish and carefully cultivated class a bit intimidating.

Her reaction to Mary Adams had a lot to do with the older woman's unconscious sense of style. In fact, Jessie couldn't ever recall seeing Erik's mother in anything more casual than wool slacks, a silk blouse and oodles of gold jewelry. Nor had she ever seen her with a single frosted hair out of place. Mary eyed Jessie's jeans and pale blue maternity sweater with obvious dismay.

"We must take you shopping," she announced, without a clue that her expression or her innuendo were insulting.

"I have plenty of clothes," Jessie protested. "Unfortunately, the baby arrived before I'd planned, so I didn't bring anything except maternity clothes along. The pants can be pinned to fit well enough."

"Not to worry," Mary said cheerfully. "I'll ask Harlan if the plane's free. The pilot can take us over to Dallas for the day. We can shop the after-Christmas sales at Neiman-Marcus. I have half a dozen things that I need to return and you certainly won't be needing those new maternity outfits we gave you now."

She shook her head, an expression of tolerant amusement on her face as she confided, "Harlan hasn't gotten my size right once in all the years we've been married. I've become used to these post-holiday exchanges."

Jessie tried again. "Maybe another day," she said a little more forcefully. Deliberately changing the subject, she asked, "Where are Jordan and Cody this morning?"

"Jordan's already flown back to Houston. He had business to attend to, or so he claimed. He's probably chasing after some new woman. I think Cody is off somewhere with his father," she said without interest.

She regarded Jessie thoughtfully. "That shade of blue isn't quite right for you. I believe something darker, perhaps a lovely royal blue, would be perfect with your eyes."

Jessie had been so certain she'd ended the subject of the shopping excursion. Apparently she hadn't. "I'm not sure I have the energy yet to keep up with you," she confessed as a last resort.

Finally something she'd said penetrated Mary's self-absorbed planning.

"Oh, my goodness, what was I thinking?" Mary said, looking chagrined. "Of course, you must be exhausted. I remember when the boys were born, I didn't even leave the hospital for a week and here it's only been a few days since Angela was born. How on earth are you managing? Young women today are much more blasé about these things than my generation was."

Since Mary's question seemed to be rhetorical and she appeared to have fallen deep into thought, Jessie concentrated on spreading jam on her perfectly toasted English muffin. She'd once wondered if the kitchen staff at White Pines had been told to toss out any that weren't an even shade of golden brown. Her own success was considerably more limited. She burned as many as she got right in the old toaster she had in her apartment.

"A nanny," Mary announced triumphantly, capturing Jessie's full attention with the out-of-the-blue remark.

"A nanny?" Jessie repeated cautiously.

"For Angela."

She'd hoped for a new tangent, but this one was pretty extreme even for Mary. "Please, it's not nec-

essary," she said firmly. "I can take care of the baby
perfectly well. Besides, you couldn't possibly find
anyone on such short notice. And I'll be going back
home next week, anyway."

"Nonsense," Mary said dismissively. "You'll be
staying right here."

When Jessie started to argue, Mary's expression
turned intractable. It was a toss-up whether Luke and
the others had gotten their stubborn streaks from
Harlan or their mother. The combined gene pool was
enough to make Jessie shudder with dread.

"I won't take no for an answer," Mary said just as
firmly. "Even if you insist on going back to that tiny
little apartment and that silly job eventually, you have
to take a few weeks of maternity leave. You'll spend it
right here, where we can look after you."

Jessie bristled at having the life she'd made for herself dismissed so casually, but she bit her tongue. She
honestly hadn't given any thought to the fact that she
was entitled to maternity leave. It was on her list of
things to worry about closer to the baby's arrival.
Angela had thrown that timetable completely off.

"I don't know how much time I'm entitled to," she
admitted.

"I believe I've heard six weeks is the norm," Mary
said distractedly, jotting herself a note on the pad she
always had at hand at breakfast for writing down the
day's chores. She dispensed them to the staff as mer-
rily as if they were checks. They weren't always re-
ceived in quite the same spirit, but Jessie doubted if
Mary noticed that.

Her mother-in-law glanced up from her notes. "Of course, three months would be better. Why don't I have Harlan call your boss and make the arrangements?" She made another note.

The thought of Harlan Adams negotiating anything with her boss gave Jessie chills. "Absolutely not. I'll make the call later today. After that I suppose we can talk more about how long I'm staying."

She gazed directly at Mary and tried to recall the precise tone of voice she'd used so successfully the evening before. "But no nanny. It wouldn't be fair to hire someone and then turn right around and fire them again."

"Well, of course not," Mary agreed far too readily. "We'll send her home with you. It will be our gift."

Jessie felt as if she were losing control of her life. "You said yourself that my apartment is tiny. When you visited, you complained you could barely turn around in it. It can hardly accommodate a live-in nanny."

Mary didn't even bat an eye at that complication. "Then we'll find you someplace larger," she said at once. She picked up her cup of tea. "If you decide to go back, of course."

"I thought we had settled that," Jessie began, then sighed. Clearly she would be better off saving this particular fight for another day. She didn't have the strength for it this morning. She stood. "I think I'll go back up and check on Angela."

"No need, Jessica. I believe Maritza's sister is sitting with her now."

She had married into a household of control freaks, Jessie decided, fighting her annoyance. Erik had quite likely been the only one in the group whose personality didn't demand that he take charge of every single situation. She had learned her lesson from observing him, though. If she didn't stand up to them, they would dismiss her opinions and her plans as no more than a minor nuisance.

"There's no need for her to stay with the baby," she told Mary forcefully. "I have a few letters to write this morning and some calls to make, so I'll be with her."

With that she turned and headed for the stairs, fully expecting yet another argument. For once, though, Mary was silent. Well, almost silent, Jessie amended. She thought she heard her mother-in-law sigh dramatically the instant she thought Jessie was out of earshot.

Back in her suite, she found a beautiful, young Mexican woman sitting right beside Angela's crib. Apparently she had taken her instructions to watch the baby quite literally, because she didn't even look away when Jessie entered the room.

"Buenos dias," Jessie said to her.

The young woman glanced her way and smiled shyly.

"Do you speak English?" Jessie asked.

"Yes."

"What's your name?"

"Lara Mendoza."

"Lara, thank you for looking after the baby. I'll stay with her now."

Lara seemed alarmed by the dismissal. "But it is my pleasure, *señora*. It is as Señora Adams wishes."

Jessie bit back a sharp retort. "It's not necessary," she insisted gently. "I'll call for you, if I need you, Lara."

Lara's sigh was every bit as heavy as the one Jessie had heard Mary utter. Apparently she was testing everyone's patience this morning.

Still, she had to admit that she was relieved to be on her own. Perhaps the decision to come to White Pines had been a bad one, after all. All of the things she'd hated most—the control, the dismissal of her opinions, the hints of disapproval—were coming back to her now.

She realized that for all of her hopes and dreams when she'd married Erik, this still wasn't her family. Jordan and Cody seemed to like her well enough. Even Harlan appeared to be fond of her. But Mary was another story. Every time her mother-in-law addressed her, Jessie couldn't help concluding that the older woman found her sadly wanting.

Suddenly she was filled with a terrible sense of despondency. Perhaps there was no place she really belonged anymore, not here and certainly not with Luke. He'd made that clear enough. Perhaps it was time she accepted the fact that she and Angela were going to have to make it entirely on their own.

A tap on the door interrupted her maudlin thoughts. She eyed the door suspiciously. She didn't think she could take another run-in with Mary just yet.

"Who is it?" she called softly, hoping not to wake the baby.

"Open the door and find out," a masculine voice said.

The sound of that unmistakable voice gave her goose bumps. She practically ran to fling open the door, relieved and elated by his timely arrival.

"Luke," she cried and propelled herself into his arms without considering his reaction.

Despite his startled grunt of surprise at her actions, he folded his arms around her and held her close. Suddenly she no longer felt nearly so alone. Breathing in the familiar masculine scent of him, crushed against his solid chest, she felt warm and protected and cherished. Those feelings might be illusions, but for now she basked in them.

After what seemed far too brief a time, Luke gently disengaged her and stepped back just far enough to examine her from head to toe. His expression hardened, as if something he saw angered him. She couldn't imagine what it could be.

"What's this?" he demanded, rubbing at the dampness on her cheeks. "What's wrong, Jessie?"

Jessie hadn't even been aware that she'd been crying before his arrival. Or maybe they were tears of joy at seeing him. Or perhaps simply the overly emotional tears of a woman who'd just given birth. She couldn't say. She just knew that at this moment she had never been more grateful to see someone in her life.

"Jessie? What's going on?" he asked as he led her away from the door and shut it behind him. A worried frown puckered his brow as he waited with obvious impatience for answers. "What has my family done to you now?"

"Nothing," she said. "Everything. Oh, Luke, they're taking over. I'm trying so damned hard not to let them. I am not a weak woman. You know that."

"No mistake about it," he agreed.

Jessie barely noticed the sudden return of a twinkle in his eye. She was too caught up in trying to explain her frustration. "But they're bulldozing right over me," she said, giving full vent to her exasperation. "They don't listen to a word I say. They don't even hear me."

To her astonishment, Luke chuckled. "Darlin', that's nothing to get all stressed out about. That's just Mother and Dad. Talk louder and stand your ground. Sooner or later, they'll get the message."

Jessie recognized the wisdom of his advice. She'd even seen how well it worked in action. She'd just lost her strength to fight there for a minute. She gazed up at Luke, tears still shimmering in her eyes, and offered a watery grin. "Quite a welcome, huh?"

He grinned. "Can't say I've ever minded having a woman hurl herself into my arms," he teased.

His gaze captured hers and held. Suddenly the teasing light in his eyes died out, replaced by something far more serious, something far more compelling. Jessie's breath snagged in her throat.

"Luke," she began huskily, then cleared her throat and tried again. "Luke, what are you doing here? Yesterday you flat-out refused to come. Did something change your mind?" She thought of the ring she'd left behind and the odd call he'd made the day before when he'd discovered it.

"I suppose you could say I came to take the pressure off you."

She regarded him uncertainly. It wasn't exactly the response she'd been anticipating. "In what way?"

He shrugged. "With me around, Daddy will be so busy trying to take charge of my life again, he won't have time to go messin' in yours."

"That's what you think," she said dismally. "Harlan could fiddle with the lives of an entire army platoon without missing a beat. As for your mother..." She sighed heavily.

Luke grinned. "Don't I just know it," he said, matching her sigh with apparent deliberation. "Maybe we should both just hide out in here for the duration."

An intriguing idea, Jessie thought. She was stunned, however, that Luke had suggested it, even in jest. Or, perhaps that was the point. Perhaps he intended to tease and taunt her as he might a younger sister, robbing her of any notions that he thought of her in any kind of sexual way. She searched his gaze for answers, but whatever emotions had been swirling there a moment before had given way to pure amusement.

"I have an idea," he said. His voice had dropped to a daring, conspiratorial note.

"What?" she asked suspiciously.

"I saw this very bored young woman sitting right outside your door. I have a feeling she would be more than glad to baby-sit for a bit."

Jessie rolled her eyes. Obviously Lara had decided to stay within shouting distance. "I'll bet," she muttered. "She's there under orders from your mother."

Luke chuckled. "Don't look a gift horse in the mouth. Let's let Lara do her thing. You and I can go to lunch."

"I just ate breakfast," Jessie protested.

"Obviously you haven't noticed the roads into town. By the time we get there, it will definitely be lunchtime."

"Won't your family be expecting you to eat lunch here? Have you even seen your father or mother yet? Or Cody?"

"Not hide nor hair of them. I snuck in the back way," he admitted. "You can help me keep it that way a little longer. Are you game?"

Jessie would have hopped a bus to nowhere if it would have gotten her away from White Pines for a little while, long enough to get back her equilibrium. A trip into town with Luke sounded perfect.

"You tell Lara," she said. "I'll get my coat."

As he started toward the door of the suite, Jessie called after him, "Luke?"

He glanced back.

"I don't have any idea what really brought you here, but I'm very glad you came."

An oddly wistful expression came over his face for an instant. It was gone in a heartbeat.

"Maybe I just heard your prayers for a knight in shining armor," he taunted. "My armor's a bit tarnished, but I can still stand up to a common enemy."

Hearing him expressing the view of Harlan and Mary that she'd been thinking to herself only a short time earlier made Jessie feel suddenly guilty. For all of their bossiness, they had always been kind to her. The huge pile of Christmas presents stacked in the corner—everything from a silver teething ring to a car seat for the baby, from a golden locket to a filmy negligee and robe for her—attested to their generosity.

"They're not that bad," she countered.

"Don't need a hero, huh? Want me to head on home, then?"

Jessie had the feeling he would be only too relieved to comply. For a multitude of reasons, she wasn't sure she could bear it if he left.

She leveled a challenging glare at him. "Just try it, Lucas. You'll have to walk through me."

He winked at her. "An interesting idea."

That wink stirred ideas in Jessie that could have gotten her arrested in some parts of the world, she was sure. Harlan and Mary would certainly have been scandalized by her thoughts. She grabbed her coat before she was tempted to act on any one of them.

As if he'd read her mind, Luke inquired lazily, "In a hurry, darlin'?"

"You have no idea," she replied in a choked voice.

"Oh, I'll bet I do." He touched a finger lightly to her lips. "Hold those thoughts."

Jessie had no problem at all complying with that rather surprising request. She doubted she could have banished them with a solid whack by a crowbar. What she couldn't comprehend to save her soul was why Luke had suddenly taken it into his head to torment her like this. Whatever his reasons, though, she intended to make the most of his presence.

He might walk away from her and from White Pines eventually, but if he went this time it wouldn't be without putting up the fight of his life for his heart. Jessie intended to claim it, this time for good.

Chapter Twelve

Luke was having a great deal of difficulty remembering what it was that had originally brought him to White Pines. Sitting across from Jessie in a booth at Rosa's Mexican Café, his mind kept wandering to that desperate, hungry kiss they had shared in his truck. Just thinking about it aroused him. She had been hot and yielding in his arms, every bit as passionate as he'd ever imagined.

Now, as he watched her gasp with each bite of Rosa's lethally hot salsa, he was just as fascinated by her passion for the spicy food. Her eyes watered. Sweat beaded on her brow. He thought she had never been more appealing, though he wondered if she was going to survive the meal.

"They have a milder version," he said, taking pity on her.

She waved off the offer. "This is delicious," she said as she grabbed her glass of water and gulped most of it down before reaching for another chip and loading it with the salsa. "The best Mexican food I've ever had. I wonder why Erik never brought me here."

Luke didn't have an answer to that, but he couldn't help being glad that they were sharing her first experience with Rosa's Café, a place he'd always preferred to the fanciest restaurants in the state. Rosa, yet another of Consuela's distant cousins, had been bossing him around since his first visit years before. Coming here felt almost more like coming home than going to White Pines. He was delighted that Jessie liked it.

In fact, he was discovering that he was captivated by her reactions to everything. It seemed to him that in many ways Jessie took a child's innocent delight in all of her surroundings. Her responses to the simplest pleasures gave him a whole new perspective on the world, as well. Each time he was with her, his jaded heart healed a bit. Each time she chipped away at his resolve not to get more deeply involved with his brother's widow.

Remembering his resolve reminded him at last of why he'd broken his vow never to return to White Pines. He had come not simply to see Jessie again and indulge his fantasies about her, but to ply her for information about her past. It was a mission from which he couldn't afford to be distracted. He wanted to give her the gift of her family before he walked out of her life.

"It doesn't bother you at all, does it?" she asked, snagging his attention.

"What?"

"The food."

"Why? Because it's hot? I grew up on Mexican food. Consuela put jalapeño peppers in everything. I'm pretty sure she ground them up and put them in our baby food."

Jessie grinned. "No wonder you're tough as nails. This stuff will definitely put hair on your chest, as my daddy used to say."

There it was, Luke thought. The perfect opening. "Tell me about your family," he suggested. "Did you always know you were adopted?"

She shook her head. "No, I didn't have a clue until I was a teenager. One night I was talking about a friend who was adopted and who'd decided to search for her birth mother, and my mother suddenly got up and ran from the room. I had no idea what I'd said to upset her so. Daddy looked at me like he'd caught me torturing a kitten or something and went rushing after her. I sat there filled with guilt without knowing why I should feel that way."

Luke couldn't begin to imagine her confusion and hurt. "Is that when they told you?"

"Later that night. I'd cleaned up the supper they'd barely touched and done the dishes when they finally came into the kitchen and told me to sit down. They looked so sad, but stoic, you know what I mean?"

Luke nodded. He'd actually seen a similar look in her face the day before, when he'd sent her away. He wondered how much of this she'd shared with Erik. A pang of pure jealousy sliced through him, and he cursed himself for being a selfish bastard, for wanting more of her than his brother had had.

Oblivious to his reaction, Jessie went on. "Anyway, they told me then that they had adopted me when I was only a few days old. They said they didn't know anything at all about my birth mother, that they hadn't wanted to know. They'd made sure the records were sealed and never looked back."

"You must have felt as if your whole world had been turned on its ear," Luke suggested.

"Worse, I think. It wasn't just that I wasn't who I'd always thought I was—Dancy and Grace Garnett's daughter. It was that they had lied to me for all those years. If you knew how Dancy and Grace preached about honesty above all else, you'd know how betrayed I felt when I learned the truth. It was as though they weren't who they'd claimed to be, either." She looked at him. "Am I making any sense here?"

"Absolutely." Since she seemed to be relieved to be sharing the story with him, Luke remained silent, hoping that would encourage her to go on.

"I begged them to let me find my biological mother, but Grace started crying and Dancy got that same accusing look on his face again."

Even now, she sounded guilt ridden, Luke noticed. "Do you realize that when you talk about them in casual conversation, you refer to them as Mother and Father, but just now, talking about that time, you instinctively started calling them by their first names?"

She seemed startled by the observation. "I suppose that's true. Like I said, I started thinking about them differently then." She gave him an imploring look. "Please, believe me when I say that no one could have had more wonderful parents. I loved them with all my heart. I grieved when they died. But something changed that night. I didn't want it to, but it did."

"Not because they were your adoptive parents, but because they'd lied."

She nodded. "The very thing they'd always told me was one of the worst sins a person could commit."

Luke felt a shudder roll through him and wondered if his own devious plan would fall into the category of lying and whether she would forgive him when she discovered what he was up to.

"But you gave up the idea of looking for your birth parents, didn't you?"

"At first I was so angry that I didn't care what they wanted, but then, after a few days, I realized how deeply hurt they would be. I told myself that they were my real parents in every way that mattered, so, yes, I dropped the idea."

"Where would you have looked?" he asked.

"Dallas, I suppose. It was the closest big city." She shrugged. "I was sixteen. This hit me out of the blue. I had no idea how to start."

"And they never told you anything more, just that you had been born in Texas?"

"Nothing." She sighed and broke the chip she was holding in two and put it aside.

When she glanced up again, Luke saw that her eyes were shimmering with unshed tears. His resolve stiffened. He would find her biological parents for her. She would have her family. She would have an identity that belonged to her, something he realized with sudden intuition was probably just as important to her as family.

No longer would she be Grace and Dancy Garnett's adopted daughter. Or Erik Adams's widow. Or even Angela Adams's mother. She would know her roots, her heritage. That, above all, was something Luke could understand. It was something no one in his family ever lost sight of. He'd been raised on tales of his ancestors and their struggles and accomplishments. They'd been held up as role models, tough in body and indomitable in spirit. Luke and his brothers had been expected to surpass their examples. The pressure had been unceasing.

It was odd, he thought. Jessie had so little family history. He sometimes thought he and his brothers had had too much. The legacy had shaped them into the men they were. He had wanted to shape his own legacy. Cody had fought to claim the one they shared. Jordan was, quite possibly, the most fiercely independent of all of them.

He reached across the table and claimed Jessie's hand. It was cold as ice. Clearly startled by his touch, she met his gaze.

"Just wanted to bring you back to the present, darlin'," he said softly.

Color rose in her cheeks. "Oh, Luke, I'm sorry. I never talk about the past like that. I can't imagine what got into me. You've probably been bored to tears."

"Anything but," he assured her, resisting the urge to run straight to the pay phone and call Jim Hill with the few bits of new information he had. He needed one last thing, though, the only thing he could think of that might help and that Jessie was sure to know, despite her doubts about so much else. He needed to find out her exact birthday. He knew how old she was—twenty-seven. And he recalled that her birthday was sometime in summer.

In fact he would never forget the celebration they'd thrown at White Pines her first year there. Erik had insisted on a real, old-fashioned Texas barbecue with neighbors coming from miles around and a live band for square dancing. He remembered every minute of it. That, in fact, was the night he'd realized that he was falling for his brother's wife, that what he'd dismissed as attraction went far deeper.

Jessie had been his partner for a spinning, whirling, breath-stealing square dance. Her cheeks had been flushed. Her bare shoulders had shimmered with a damp sheen of perspiration. Her lush lips had been parted, inviting a kiss. He had obliged before he'd realized he was going to do it. The quick, impulsive kiss had been briefer than a heartbeat, but it had shaken him to his core. Jessie had looked as if she'd been poleaxed.

The band had shifted gears just then and played a slow dance. Jessie had drifted into his arms, innocently relaxing against him, oblivious he was certain to the fact that his body was pulsing with sudden, urgent need. Desperate to keep her from discovering just how badly he wanted her, he had spotted Erik across the dance floor and maneuvered them into his brother's path. Erik had been only too eager to claim his wife.

If there had been regret in Jessie's eyes, Luke had blinded himself to it. He'd taken off right after that dance and from that day on he'd steered as far away from Jessie as he possibly could without drawing notice.

Glancing at her, he wondered if she recalled that night as vividly as he did. Bringing up the memory was one way to learn the last piece of information he figured he could get for the detective—or so he told himself.

"Hey, darlin', do you recall that shindig we threw for your birthday your first year at White Pines?"

Her blue eyes sparkled at once. "Goodness, yes. I'd never had such a lavish birthday party. Your parents actually had a dance floor installed under the stars, remember?"

"Oh, I remember," he said, his voice dropping a seductive notch.

"I'd never square danced before."

"You sure took to it."

"It was exhilarating," she said softly, and her eyes met his, her expression nostalgic.

If she was saying more than the obvious, Luke couldn't be sure. He decided for his own sanity it would be best to steer away from the minefield of any more intimate memories.

"Was that July or August? All I remember was how hot it was." Of course, he conceded to himself, his memory of the temperature might have had nothing to do with the weather. Jessie could have had his blood steaming with a look back then. She still could, he admitted. Air-conditioning hadn't been manufactured that could cool him off in her presence.

"August second," she said. "It was the day before my birthday."

That nailed it down, Luke thought, rather proud of himself. He glanced at his watch, then slid from the booth. "Excuse me a second, Jessie. There's a phone call I was supposed to make. I just now remembered it."

She regarded him oddly, but said nothing. Feeling like a sneak, Luke practically raced to the phone booth. He reached the detective on the third ring.

"I was able to come up with a little more information," he said and gave him what he had. "Does that help at all?"

"Some," Hill said. "I ran the name through the computer after we talked, just to see if anything turned up based on what you had this morning."

Luke sucked in a breath. "And?"

"Nothing much beyond the usual, social security number, credit rating, that kind of thing. There was one thing I found a little odd, though."

"What?"

"Looks to me as if she's been investigated before. There are some inquiries on the credit history."

"Couldn't that have been for a car loan or a job reference or something?"

"Possibly. It just didn't seem to track that way."

"How recently?"

"A few years back."

Luke felt his heart begin to thud dully. "In the fall?"

"As a matter of fact, yes. Most of the inquiries seemed to be around September or October."

Erik and Jessie had been married on November first. Her name had started coming up at White Pines only a month or two before as someone about whom Erik was serious.

"Do you know something about that?" Hill asked.

"Not for certain, but I'd put my money on Daddy," Luke said, fighting his anger. He'd known that Harlan suspected Jessie's motives in marrying Erik, but he'd had no idea he'd gone so far as to check her out. "My guess is that Harlan was doing some checking before Erik and Jessie got married. He probably wanted to be sure that the Adams name wasn't about to be sullied or that she wasn't going to take Erik for a fortune."

The detective didn't react to Luke's explanation except to say, "Maybe you can get the information you're after from your father, then. He was probably pretty thorough. Do you want me to wait until you check it out?"

"No, get started. Even Daddy probably couldn't bust his way into sealed adoption records."

"What makes you think you can?"

"Because you're going to tell me exactly how to go about it, and then I'm going to tell Jessie. She's probably the only one who can get through the legal red tape."

"If she wants to," Hill reminded him.

Luke thought of the sad expression he'd seen on her face earlier. "She'll want to," he said with certainty.

"She might not like what she finds."

"I'll be with her every step of the way," he vowed. "It'll be okay."

"You're the boss," the detective said. "I'll be in touch as soon as I have anything. Where will I find you?"

"At White Pines."

"Home for the holidays?"

"Exactly," Luke said dryly. "Just your typical family get-together."

It would be a lot less typical when he cornered his father about having Jessie investigated before the wedding. He was filled with indignation on her behalf. In fact, he might very well do something he'd been itching to do for years. He might wring Harlan's scrawny old neck.

Luke's expression looked as if it had been carved in stone when he came back from making that phone call. Whatever it had been about, the call had obviously upset him.

Jessie watched his profile warily on the ride home, wondering if she should try to probe for an explanation for his change in mood. She supposed she ought to be used to his sullen silences, but having caught a few tantalizing glimpses of the other, gentler side of his nature, she wasn't sure she could bear this return to an old demeanor, an old distance between them.

"Bad news?" she inquired eventually.

"You could say that," he said tersely.

"Can I help?"

He glanced her way. "Nope. I'll take care of it."

Jessie's gaze narrowed. "You jumped in this morning when you saw I had a problem," she reminded him. "Why won't you let me return the favor?"

"Because I can solve this myself."

"I could have solved my problem myself, but that didn't prevent you from butting in, because you cared."

Luke's gaze settled on her and his mouth curved into the beginnings of a smile. "You saying you care, Jessie?"

"Well, of course I do," she said hotly. "Luke, you know how I feel about you..." At the warning look in his eyes, her voice trailed off. Then, irritated with him and herself, she added determinedly, "And about what you did for me and Angela."

"Let's not start that again."

"Well, dammit, it's not something I'm ever likely to forget."

"Stop cursing. It's out of character."

She lost patience with all the verbal tap dancing. "Lucas, you are the most exasperating, mule-headed man it has ever been my misfortune to know. It's no wonder I'm cursing."

He grinned at her outburst. "I care about you, too," he conceded, his voice gentler. "If I really needed help with this, Jessie, I swear you'd be the first person I'd turn to."

Ridiculously pleased, she said, "Really?"

"Cross my heart."

"So does it have something to do with the ranch?"

He laughed. "Give you an inch and you go for the whole damned mile, don't you?"

"You know a better way to get what you want?"

An oddly defeated expression passed across his face. "No, darlin', I can't say that I do."

"Luke?"

"Drop it, Jessica. There's nothing for you to worry about." He glanced at her. "Except maybe how you're going to bring Mother and Daddy to heel."

She heaved a sigh. "I'd rather tackle your problem."

"No," he said with a grim note in his voice. "I can just about guarantee that you wouldn't."

Before Jessie could respond to that cryptic remark, he'd parked the fancy four-wheel-drive car in front of the garage and climbed out. Before she could move, he had her door open. He reached out, circled her waist with his hands and lifted her down from the high vehicle.

He was close enough that she could feel his warmth, close enough that his breath whispered against her cheek. She would have given anything to stay just that way, but the reality was they were at White Pines and there were far too many prying eyes.

Besides, judging from the grim, determined set of Luke's jaw, he would not have allowed it.

"Come on, darlin'. Let's go show 'em who's in charge of our lives."

"I was thinking maybe I'd slip away and take a nap," Jessie said wistfully.

"Resting up before the big battle," Luke noted. "A good idea."

"You could do the same," she suggested daringly, casting a sly look up at him. If the way his jaw was working was any indication, he did not mistake the seductive intent of the invitation.

"Darlin', believe me, that would be a declaration of war," he advised her.

Jessie was up for it. And Luke, she knew with every fiber of her being, was tempted. She winked at him. "One of these days you're going to take me up on it," she taunted him.

"Not in this lifetime," he said emphatically.

Jessie just grinned. She had a feeling deep inside that he was wrong. He was going to cave in far sooner than he thought. She could hardly wait.

Chapter Thirteen

With Jessie resting in her suite, Luke paced up and down in his own, trying to cool off before confronting his father with what he'd discovered. Walking into a room and hurling accusations after months of separation would hardly get their relationship back on track. Still, he couldn't help wondering if Harlan made a habit of investigating any woman with whom any of his sons were involved. If that were the case, Jordan and Cody would probably send him into bankruptcy. Luke took a sort of grim pleasure in the prospect. He'd often wondered if his father would ever have to pay the price for his attempted control of his sons.

When he finally considered his temper calm and his approach reasonable, he bounded down the stairs two at a time and headed straight for Harlan's office.

He found his father seated behind a massive desk piled high with files and spread sheets. Wearing a pair of reading glasses, he was squinting at a computer screen, a sour expression on his once-rugged face. Except for the glasses and perhaps a new wrinkle or two, the scene of his father engrossed in work was so familiar that it made Luke's heart ache.

The glasses and the faint signs of aging, though, reminded him of just how long he'd been away. It wasn't just since Erik's death, but all the years since he'd declared his independence from Harlan's manipulations and moved to his own ranch. He wondered how many other subtle changes there had been since he'd gone.

Harlan glanced up at Luke's entrance. "So, there you are," he said.

His pleasure at seeing Luke was betrayed by his eyes, even though his tone was neutral. He almost sounded uncertain, Luke thought with surprise. It was a far cry from the usual arrogance. He couldn't help welcoming the change.

"About time," Harlan grumbled, his tone more in character. "I wondered where the hell you'd disappeared to. Your mother didn't even know you'd arrived. Wouldn't have known it myself except one of the trucks was missing."

"I had an errand in town. Jessie came along and we had lunch," he added with his usual touch of defiance. Even after all this time, it was a knee-jerk reaction, he realized with a sense of chagrin. If his father commented on the weather, Luke found some reason to counter his claim.

His father nodded, ignoring the testiness. "Fresh air probably did her good. She looked a mite peaked to me last night."

"She just had a baby," Luke reminded him.

His father's expression finally shifted to permit a small hint of approval. "Cute little thing, isn't she?" he said with a note of pride. "Looks like an Adams."

"I was thinking she looked like Jessie," Luke countered, just to be contrary... again.

Harlan shrugged, not rising to the bait. "Who can tell at that age?" he admitted. "You boys all looked exactly alike when you were born." His expression turned thoughtful. "Not a one of you turned out the same, though, in looks or personality. I never could make sense of how that happened."

"We all got your stubborn streak, though," Luke reminded him.

Harlan chuckled at that. "I like to blame that particular trait on your mama. Makes her crazy."

"I can imagine."

Harlan settled back in his chair and studied Luke intently. "You look tired. Why'd you really come home, son? You have something on your mind?"

"I just thought it was about time for a visit," Luke replied noncommittally.

"Your mother's going to be mighty glad to see you."

Luke doubted it. Mary Adams was too caught up in her own social whirl and in her husband to pay much mind to the comings and goings of her sons. He was more interested in his father's reaction. They had never parted without some sort of petty squabble, probably just the clash of two strong wills. Since Erik's death the tension had been greater than ever.

"And you?" he asked, watching his father's expression closely.

His father seemed taken aback by the question. "That goes without saying," he said at once. "This is your home, boy. Always will be."

Luke sighed, relieved yet still incapable of fully believing the easy answer. "I wasn't so sure you felt that way after the way Erik died," he said cautiously. "It's understandable that you might blame me for what happened."

"Is that what's kept you away from here?"

Luke shrugged. "Part of it."

"Well, you were wrong. Your brother died because he was a reckless fool," his father snapped angrily, "not because of anything you did."

Luke was startled by the depth of emotion. He suspected there was a heavy measure of guilt behind the anger, but hell would freeze over before Harlan would admit to it. Still, the reaction worked to his advantage. With his father's usual control snapped, it seemed like the perfect moment to get an honest answer from him.

"I wonder how he would have felt if he'd known you had Jessie investigated," Luke inquired casually, his gaze pinned to his father's face. "It might have given him the gumption to go after the life he really wanted."

Harlan's skin turned ashen. "What the devil do you know about that?" he demanded indignantly, unsuspectingly confirming Luke's suspicions. "And what business is it of yours, if I did?"

Luke refused to be drawn into an argument over ethics, morality or just plain trust. He had his own agenda here. "Find out anything interesting?" he inquired lightly.

"Nothing worth stopping the wedding over, which you obviously knew already." He leveled a look at Luke. "Like I asked before, what business is this of yours? It happened a long time ago. If anyone should have told me to mind my own business, it was Erik, but he never said peep."

"Maybe because he was too damned trusting to suspect you'd do something like that. I'm not nearly so gullible where you're concerned. I know how manipulative you can be. I like Jessie. I don't like to think that you don't trust her."

"Is that it?" Harlan demanded with a penetrating look. "Or is it something more?"

Luke felt as if he were standing at the edge of a mine field with one foot already in the air for his next fateful step. "Like what?"

"Like maybe your interest in her is personal."

"Well, of course it's personal," he snapped, hoping to divert his father from making too much of his defense of Jessie by admitting straight out that he cared for her as he would for any other family member. It was a risky tactic. It appeared his father had been far more attuned to the undercurrents around White Pines than he'd realized.

"She's my sister-in-law," he pointed out. "She just delivered my niece in my bed a few days ago. I'd say that gives me cause to take an interest in her."

"And that's all there is to it?" Harlan inquired, skepticism written all over his face.

"Of course." Luke uttered the claim with what he hoped was enough vehemence. His father still didn't exactly look as if he believed him, but to Luke's relief he appeared willing to let the matter drop.

"You found out she was adopted, didn't you?" Luke prodded.

"Already knew that. Erik told us."

"Did you find out anything about her family?"

"Now who's asking too many questions?"

Luke scowled at him. "Just answer me. I have my reasons for asking."

"So did I," Harlan said testily.

Luke stood. "Never mind. I can see this was a waste of time."

"Oh, for goodness sakes, settle down. Yes, I found out about her family. They were good, decent, church-going people. Paid their bills on time. Gave her a good education. There was nothing to find fault with there."

"I meant her biological family."

An expression of pure frustration spread across his father's rough-hewn features. "Couldn't get any-where with that. Didn't seem worth chasing after, once I'd met her. My gut instinct is never wrong and it told me right off that Jessie's honest as they come. If I hadn't known it before, there was no mistaking it when she walked away from here without a cent after

Erik died. She's a gutsy little thing, too stubborn for her own good, if you ask me."

"An interesting assessment coming from you," Luke observed.

Harlan's expression turned sheepish. "So it is."

Luke decided he'd better get out of his father's office before Harlan picked up the issue of Luke's feelings for Jessie and pursued it. He'd diverted his father once, but Harlan was too damned perceptive for Luke to keep his emotions hidden from him for long. A few probing questions, a few evasive answers and the truth would be plain as day.

"I think I'll go hunt down Mother," he told his father.

"I believe you'll find her in the parlor reading or planning some social schedule," Harlan said with a grimace. He turned back to his computer and sighed. "You know anything about these danged things?"

"Enough to get by," Luke said.

"Maybe you could give me a few pointers later. At the rate I'm going, this year's records won't even be programmed before next year."

Surprised by the request, Luke nodded. "I'd be happy to." It was the first time he could ever recall his father admitting that one of his sons might have an expertise he didn't. That single request went a long way toward mending fences, hinting that perhaps they could finally find a new footing for their relationship, one of equals. Respect was all he'd ever really craved from his father. He'd known he had his love, but true respect had been far harder to come by.

Just as Luke reached the door, his father called after him. "It really is good to have you home again, son. This house was built for the whole family. Never realized how empty it would be one day."

Luke felt an unexpected lump form in his throat. He'd discovered the same thing about his own house recently, as well. For a few brief days it had felt like a home. "Thanks, Daddy," he said. "It's good to be here."

Oddly enough, he realized as he walked away, it was true. It was unexpectedly good to be home. He wondered just how much of that could be attributed to Jessie's presence upstairs and whether from now on "home" to him would always be wherever she was.

That night as he dressed for dinner, Luke conceded that his prediction of his mother's reaction to seeing him had been right on target. She had been superficially pleased when she'd greeted him, but within minutes she'd been distracted by a flurry of phone calls from friends confirming holiday plans. He'd been only too glad to escape to his suite, where he waited impatiently for some news from Jim Hill. He doubted his mother had even noticed when he left the parlor.

Upstairs, he spent a restless hour wishing he still had a right to head out to his father's barns and work the horses. He needed some hard exercise to combat the stress of being home again, of being so close to a woman he hungered for and couldn't have. His shoulders ached with tension. His nerves were on edge. He would have gone out and chopped wood, if he hadn't seen a woodpile big enough to last till spring.

He supposed the real truth was that he'd been feeling tense and out of sorts ever since Jessie had appeared on his doorstep. It was as if he were being ripped apart inside, torn between desire and honor. If he'd thought his emotions were frayed at his ranch, he realized now that the necessity for watching every word, every glance while under his father's roof only compounded the problem. His conscience, never something he'd worried too much about before Erik's marriage to Jessie, was taking a royal beating.

Eventually he tired of pacing. Worn out by tangling with his own thoughts, he started back downstairs. Outside Jessie's door, he heard Angela crying and Lara's unsuccessful attempts to quiet her. He hesitated, wondering where Jessie was. Perhaps she had already gone downstairs.

He tapped on the door and opened it. The young Mexican girl, her cheeks flushed, her hair mussed, was frantically rocking the crying baby. The jerky movement was not having a soothing effect. Quite the contrary, in fact.

"What's the problem?"

"I cannot get her to sleep," Lara whispered, sounding panicked. "No matter what I do, she cries."

"Where's Jessie?"

"With the *señora*."

"Has the baby been fed?"

"*Sí.* Only a short time ago."

Luke crossed the room in a few quick strides, then reached down and took the baby from Lara. She fit into his arms as if she belonged there, her warm little body snuggling against his chest. Her gulping cries turned to whimpers almost at once.

"Shh," he whispered. "It's your Uncle Luke, sweet pea. What's with all the noise? Were you feeling abandoned there for a minute?" He glanced at Lara and saw that an expression of relief had spread across her face. "How was she while we were out this afternoon?"

"Like an angel, Señor Luke. She slept most of the time. I thought she would go to sleep again as soon as she had eaten."

Luke rubbed the baby's back. A tiny hand waved in the air, then settled against his cheek. As if she found the contact familiar and comforting, she quieted at once. That strange sense of completeness stole over him again.

Luke made a decision. "Lara, why don't you take a break for a few hours. I think our little angel ought to join the rest of us for dinner."

"But *la señora* said ..."

Luke tried to recall exactly how many times he'd heard his mother's edicts repeated in just that way by Consuela, by his father, even his teachers. Mary Adams's influence had been felt everywhere in his life, at least when she chose to exert it. "Let me worry about my mother. Have your dinner. Go on out for the evening. We can manage here."

"*Sí*, if that is your wish," she said with obvious reluctance.

"It is," he assured her.

He found a soft pink baby blanket, obviously a new addition since he doubted there would have been anything pink in the assortment of items his mother had saved from her sons. Wrapping Angela loosely in the blanket, he cradled her in one arm and gathered a few spare diapers and a bottle with his other hand. He eyed a can of baby powder, debated a couple of toys, but abandoned them when he couldn't figure out how to pick them up.

"Remind me to get you one of those fancy carry things," he told the baby, who regarded him with wide-eyed fascination. "I don't have enough hands to carry this much paraphernalia. Things were a whole lot less complicated at my house, before you got outfitted with the best supplies money could buy."

Angela gurgled her agreement.

"You know what I love most about you, sweet pea? You go along with everything I say. Be careful with all that adoration, though. It'll give a guy a swelled head. I don't want to give away any trade secrets. After all, we men should really stick together when it comes to women, but for you I'll make an exception. If there's any heartbreaking to be done, I want you to be the one who does it. You need advice about some jerk, you come to me. Is it a deal?"

The baby cooed on cue. Luke grinned.

"You understood every word, didn't you? Well, now that we've settled how you should go about dealing with men, let's go find your mama and your grandparents. Not that I'm so crazy about sharing you, you understand, but the truth is I'm not always going to be around. You need to have other folks you can count on, too. Your mama's one of the best. And nobody on earth will protect you from harm any better than your granddaddy. He's fierce when it comes to taking care of his own. Just don't let him bully you.''

Angela yawned.

"Okay, okay, I get the message. I'm boring you. Let's go, then.''

Downstairs, he located the rest of the family in the parlor. He found the varying reactions fascinating—and telling. His mother looked vaguely dismayed by the sight of Angela in his arms, just as she had when any of her own children had slipped downstairs during a grown-up party. His father grinned, unable to hide his pleasure or his pride, just as he had when showing off his sons to company. Jessie seemed resigned at the sight of her daughter comfortably settled against Luke's chest.

"Where on earth is Lara?" his mother demanded at once. "I am paying that girl to look after the baby.''

Before Luke could say a word, Jessie jumped in. "Don't blame Lara. I suspect your son is responsible for this. Is that right, Luke?''

Luke shrugged, refusing to apologize. "She was crying.''

"Babies cry," his mother said irritably. "Picking them up will only spoil them.''

"Oh, for goodness sakes, Mary, she's a newborn," Harlan countered. "There's nothing wrong with giving her a little extra attention. Besides, I want to get to know my first grandbaby. Bring her here, Luke.''

He eagerly held out his arms. Luke placed the baby in them and wondered at the oddly bereft feeling that instantly came over him. He moved over and took a seat by Jessie, gravitating almost unconsciously to her warmth as an alternative to the strange sort of serenity he felt when holding the baby.

As soon as he sat down, though, he realized his mistake. Jessie represented more than warmth. She exuded heat and passion, at least to him. His body responded at once, predictably and with the kind of urgency he hadn't known since his teens.

"Sherry, Lucas?" his mother asked.

"Hmm?" he murmured distractedly.

"She's asking if you would like a drink," Jessie explained as if she were translating a foreign language. There was a look of knowing amusement in her eyes he couldn't mistake.

"No thanks," he said.

"I'm very surprised to see you here, Lucas," his mother commented.

"But we're delighted, aren't we, Mary?" his father said, a warning note in his voice.

His mother seemed startled by the sharp tone. "Well, of course, we are. I'm just surprised, that's all. He hasn't been here for months. And," she added pointedly, "he told me quite plainly that he couldn't get here over the holidays. As I recall, he told you the same thing just yesterday."

Luke refused to be drawn into a quarrel. "Plans change," he said.

"Will you be staying long?" his mother asked.

"Mary!" Harlan protested. "You'll make the boy think we'd rather he stayed home."

His mother flushed. "Well, of course, I didn't mean that. For goodness sakes, Harlan, I was just trying to think ahead and make some plans. I was wondering if we should have another party, perhaps for New Year's Eve."

Luke shuddered at the thought. "Not on my account," he said with absolute sincerity.

"I think a quiet celebration is more in order this year," Harlan said, regarding him with something that might have been understanding. "I think we had enough chaos around here last night to last till next year."

"Chaos?" Mary repeated, red patches of indignation in her cheeks. "I worked for weeks to make sure that we had a lovely party for our friends on Christmas and you thought it was chaos?"

Harlan sighed. "I didn't mean any disrespect, dear. Your parties are always well attended. They're the high point of the social season around the whole state of Texas. Everyone knows that. I just think one is enough." As if he sensed that his fancy verbal footwork hadn't yet placated her, he added, "Besides, I know first-hand how much the planning takes out of you."

Mary sighed heavily, her expression put-upon. "I suppose a quiet family occasion would be nice for a change. Perhaps for once Jordan and Cody can be persuaded to leave their current paramours at home."

"I doubt that will be a problem," his father said. "Jordan claims to be fed up with the social whirl and Cody's trying to put a damper on Melissa's enthusiasm for a spring wedding. I suspect they'll be happy to come alone."

"That was certainly the impression I got from them, too," Jessie chimed in. "I never thought I'd see the day when those two would turn up anywhere without a woman, but they seemed almost relieved to be on their own last night."

After the initial awkwardness and minor bickering, the rest of the evening settled into something astonishingly comfortable. Dinner passed quickly with quiet conversation about old friends and plans for the next few days of the holidays.

"The McAllisters' annual party is tomorrow night," Mary reminded them. She looked at Luke and Jessie. "I'm sure you'll both want to come."

"Not me," Jessie said at once. "I'm not quite up to partying yet, but the rest of you go."

Luke noticed that Jessie claimed a lack of energy only when it suited her purposes. She'd always hated the stuffy McAllisters and the collection of rich and powerful they dutifully assembled periodically to prove their own worth to the neighbors.

"I believe I'll stay here, too," he said, studiously avoiding Jessie's gaze.

His mother opened her mouth to protest, but to his surprise, his father defended his decision. "Mary, leave him be. If it were up to me, I'd stay home, too, but I know you won't have it."

"Well, for goodness sakes, it's social occasions like this that make the kind of business contacts you need," his mother grumbled. "I should think Luke would be aware of that, as well."

Luke settled back in his chair, his decision reinforced by his father's surprising understanding. "I prefer to make my business contacts in an office, Mother. That way there's no confusing my intent. As I recall, the last time I tried to do business at one of these social occasions, Henry Lassiter thought I was going to trade a herd of cattle for his daughter's hand in marriage."

Next to him, Jessie choked back a laugh. Her eyes sparkled with undisguised merriment. "How on earth did you extricate yourself from that?"

"Thank goodness I didn't have to," he said, laughing at the memory. "Janice Lassiter was as appalled as I was. She told her father in no uncertain terms that she was not a piece of property he could trade in to get a prize bull and a few cows. I have to admit I found her a bit more intriguing after she said that."

To his surprise his mother's mouth curved into a smile. "You never told us that story."

"Of course not," Luke said. "Do you realize how embarrassing it was to realize that I'd made some innocent remark that got mistaken for a marriage proposal? It's not something a man wants getting around."

Jessie leaned close and whispered, "There are some women who might even take you up on an innocent remark even without the offer of the cattle. Those are the ones you really have to watch your step with."

Luke shifted and stared at her, his blood suddenly thundering in his veins. He could feel his cheeks flush and prayed that his very observant father was watching something else at the moment. If Luke meant anything at all to Angela, who was sound asleep in her grandfather's arms, the little munchkin would wake up and start screaming right now to divert attention.

She didn't, which meant he had to hide his reactions as best he could.

Why had he never noticed that sweet, demure Jessie was a master of torment? She must have had poor Erik in a daze from the day they'd met. Or perhaps his brother had been made of sterner stuff than he'd ever realized.

"Watch yourself, darlin'," he murmured in an aside he hoped couldn't be overheard. "You're just begging for trouble."

Jessie turned her deceptively innocent gaze on him. "Who's going to give it to me, Lucas?"

Good question. For him to tangle with her in the way he longed to, the way she was taunting him to, he was the one who would be in real trouble. Up to his neck in it, as a matter of fact, and drowning fast.

Chapter Fourteen

If it weren't for the half dozen servants scattered around, Luke and Jessie would have had the house to themselves the following evening, once his parents had gone off to the McAllisters' party. For some reason, Jessie found being alone with Luke at White Pines oddly intimate and very disconcerting. Acknowledging her feelings for Luke at his ranch had been one thing. Admitting them here, where she and Erik had spent their entire married life, was something else entirely.

Frankly, she was still surprised that Luke had conspired to be alone with her. When she'd left his ranch, she had been all but certain she would never see him again unless she arranged it. Now, not only had he followed her to White Pines, he seemed unwilling to let her out of his sight. She couldn't believe it was because he'd had a change of heart about their relationship. He was still jumpy as a june bug around her. To be truthful, she wasn't much better.

Sitting across from Luke in the huge, formal dining room, with the table set with fancy china, sterling silver and fine crystal, Jessie felt as if the atmosphere were suddenly charged with electricity. In his kitchen she had been comfortable, even sure of herself. Here she felt as if she were on a first, very nerve-racking date. She wondered if he felt the same uncertainty, the same shivery anticipation.

If he did, it wasn't apparent, she decided with some regret. He'd worn slacks and a white dress shirt, left open at the throat just enough to reveal a sexy whorl of crisp, dark hair and tanned skin. With his hair neatly combed, his cheeks freshly shaved, he looked as confident as Jordan, as sexy as Cody and as at ease as Erik. The combination was enough to make her palms sweat.

Luke lifted his glass of wine and took a slow sip, his gaze never leaving her face. The intensity of that look was deliberate. There was no mistake about it. Jessie could feel her cheeks flush. Her pulse skittered wildly.

"Everything okay?" he inquired in a lazy drawl that sent fire dancing through her veins.

"Of course," she responded in a choked voice. "Why?"

"You look a little . . . feverish."

Oh, sweet heaven, she thought desperately, wishing she could pat her cheeks with a napkin dipped in the crystal goblet of ice water. The man was deliberately turning the tables on her. She swallowed hard and searched her soul for the confidence to play his game and win. "No," she said eventually, her voice shaking. "I'm fine."

He nodded politely, but there was a knowing gleam in his eyes. "If you say so."

"I do," she said adamantly.

"Okay."

Fortunately, Maritza came in with the main course just then—beef Wellington. "It is your favorite, Señor Luke, *sí?*"

Luke grinned at her, his attention diverted at last. Jessie used the reprieve to draw in a deep breath and surreptitiously fan herself with her napkin.

"Absolutely," he told the housekeeper. "And not even Consuela does beef Wellington better than you do."

"I will not tell her you said so," Maritza said, her cheeks rosy with pleasure at the compliment.

"Thank you," Luke said, his expression absolutely serious. "She'd put me on a diet of canned soup for a month, if she found out."

When the housekeeper had retreated to the kitchen, Jessie said, "You're very kind to her."

He seemed surprised by the comment. "Why wouldn't I be? She's terrific. The whole family is. Did you know that Rosa who owns the café we went to is another cousin? I believe Lara is Rosa's daughter or maybe she's a second cousin. I've lost track of all the connections."

"And you're nice to all of them." Seeing his skepticism, Jessie tried to analyze what she'd seen in their rapport. "I can't explain exactly," she finally admitted. "It's not that you're just polite, that you say what's expected. You genuinely appreciate what they do. I'm sure that's why Consuela chose to go with you when you left White Pines. I suspect you make her feel like part of the family, while your mother treated her like hired help."

Luke shrugged off the compliment. "Consuela is family to me," he said with surprising feeling. "She's the one who really raised me, raised all of us, for that matter. Mother's single goal in life was to make Daddy's life easier, to give him whatever he wanted. She gave him four sons, then did everything she could to see that we stayed out of his way. If I'm ever fortunate enough to have children, I made a promise to myself that they will never feel the way we felt as kids, as if we were a nuisance to be tolerated."

Jessie was appalled by the assessment, by the trace of bitterness in his voice. Obviously his resentments ran deeper than she'd ever realized.

"Your father certainly never treated any of you that way as far as I could tell," she argued. "He's obviously very proud of all of you."

Luke's expression was doubtful. "You can say that after the way he manipulated Erik, the way he's always tried to control the rest of us?"

Jessie found herself smiling at the concept that anyone on earth could manipulate or control Luke. "I don't see that he exactly has you under his thumb."

"Because I rebelled."

"Don't you suppose the struggle to become your own man made you stronger?"

His gaze narrowed. "What's your point?"

"That if Harlan had made it easy for you, you might not have fought half so hard to get your own way. All of this could have been yours. You would have had a nice, comfortable life without really struggling for it."

"Are you saying he deliberately battled with us over every little thing just to make us fight back?"

Jessie shrugged, refusing to spell it out any more clearly. She wanted him to look at his past from a fresh perspective and draw his own conclusion. "You know Harlan better than I do."

Luke's expression grew thoughtful. "I never thought about it that way before," he conceded. "I always wanted my own place. I didn't want to follow in his footsteps and simply claim what he'd already built. The harder he fought to keep me here, the harder I fought to go."

"And you succeeded in making the break," she pointed out. "You have a successful ranch of your own now, one you can be especially proud of because you know it's the result of your own hard work, isn't that right?"

He nodded slowly. "Jordan made the break, as well. He and Daddy used to stay up half the night fighting over his future. Daddy was fed up with him wildcatting at oil wells all over hell and gone. Told him it was time to settle down back here. Swore he'd cut him out of the will, if he didn't stay."

He paused, then suddenly grinned. "I just remembered something. I was here the night Jordan packed his bags and stormed out to move to Houston. He told

Daddy he could take his inheritance and shove it. I came down when I heard all the commotion and found Daddy standing at a window watching him go. There were tears in his eyes and the strangest look on his face.''

"What kind of look?" Jessie asked.

"I realize now that it was satisfaction, maybe even that pride you're so sure he feels for us. He was actually glad that Jordan was going after his dream," he said, a note of astonishment in his voice. "Jordan even admitted to me later that he'd had an awfully easy time landing his first desk job in the oil business. He always had a hunch that Daddy had made a call or two."

"Could be," Jessie said. "Too bad he hasn't tackled Jordan's social life. It's time he settled down. I think he's finally ready."

"Really?" Luke shook his head, clearly bemused by the discoveries he was making once he looked past those deeply ingrained resentments. "That would be something to see. I think Jordan's going to surprise us all when he finally falls in love."

"What about Cody? How did Harlan deal with him?" Jessie asked.

"In his heart, Cody was the one who always wanted White Pines," Luke said. "Unlike Jordan or me, Daddy kept pushing him toward the door. The harder he pushed, the more Cody dug in his heels and made himself indispensable around here. The next thing we knew he'd built himself a little house down the road and was acting as foreman."

Three brothers, Jessie thought, all a little stronger because Harlan had had the wisdom to make them fight for their choices in life, rather than handing them a future on a silver platter.

And then there was Erik.

"Erik was the only one the technique backfired with," she said softly. "He was never like the rest of you. He was gentle, eager to please. You said yourself the other day that he was the diplomat. Whenever Harlan pushed him, he backed down, tried to find a middle ground, hoping to win his father's approval. Instead, Harlan just grew more and more impatient with him."

Luke reached for her hand. Jessie supposed he meant it only as a gesture of comfort, but it made her senses spin. She couldn't have pulled away, though, if her life had depended on it. Fortunately, she supposed, Luke broke off the contact all too soon.

"I suppose the real skill in parenting is understanding each child's personality," Luke said thoughtfully. "Daddy said just last night how amazed he was at how different we were. Maybe if he'd recognized that sooner, Erik wouldn't have suffered so, trying to be something he wasn't. And you wouldn't have lost him."

Jessie took a deep breath and met Luke's gaze. It was time to tell him everything and see where it led them. "I suspect I was destined to lose him one way or another. At least this way he never had to lose me to another man."

Luke choked on the sip of wine he'd just taken. His eyes watered as he stared at her with astonishment written all over his face. "What are you saying?" he demanded.

Jessie drew in a deep breath. She wasn't going to let him mistake her meaning with subtleties. "That I was in love with you long before Erik died," she admitted boldly.

Luke was shaking his head before she completed the sentence. "Don't say that," he protested.

"Why not? It's true." She leveled a gaze into his troubled eyes. "Why do you think I left here after Erik died?"

"Because you couldn't bear to be around me, knowing I'd caused his death," Luke said.

Jessie decided she'd already opened the door. It was time to walk through it.

"No," she told him softly, but adamantly. "Because I was filled with guilt over my feelings for you. From the day Erik and I moved into White Pines, I felt this connection to you. I didn't want it. I couldn't explain it. I certainly could never have acted on it, but it was there, just under the surface, tormenting me."

Tears welled up in her eyes, spilled down her cheeks. "You have no idea how guilty I felt when he died. A tiny part of me was actually glad that I would never have to make a decision to leave him. I don't think I could have, no matter how badly I wanted to. I could never have hurt him that way. For all of his weaknesses, Erik was good to me. He deserved better than he got from me. He deserved my whole heart, instead of just a piece of it."

She thought back to the few moments she'd had with Erik at the hospital after Luke had come to tell her that her husband was dying. Alert for just a heartbeat, he'd turned that gentle, understanding gaze of his on her.

"Be happy, Jessie," he'd whispered, clutching her hand in his.

"Not without you," she'd insisted, as the life slowly seeped from his body with each weakening beat of his heart.

He'd squeezed her hand fiercely. "Tell him, Jessie." Then more emphatically, he'd said, "Tell Luke."

At first she hadn't realized what he meant. "What?" she'd pleaded. "Tell Luke what?"

He'd struggled for air, then managed to choke out two words. "Love him."

"Of course, I will tell him that you love him," she'd soothed, caressing his cheek.

He'd smiled faintly at that. "Not me. You."

Remembering how stunned she'd been, how consumed with guilt, Jessie thought no man had ever displayed more love, more generosity than Erik when he'd clung to her hand and said, "'S okay, Jessie."

"Oh, Erik, forgive me," she'd pleaded.

That sweet smile spread across his face one last time. "Nothing to forgive," he'd whispered. "I love you."

She gazed across the table at Luke and wondered how much she should tell him about Erik's final words. Would they free him to love her?

Or, as they had with her, would they merely renew his own deeply ingrained sense of guilt? Knowing that Erik had guessed how they felt about each other, even if neither of them had ever acted on those feelings, was a heavy burden. She could attest to that. It had driven her from White Pines.

In the end she kept silent and the moment to confide passed.

"You're not in love with me," Luke said sharply, cutting into her reverie.

Jessie's head snapped up. She almost choked on the bubble of hysterical laughter that formed in her throat. He seemed to think by saying it enough, he could make it true.

"Lucas, that is not for you to say."

He slammed his glass of wine onto the table with so much force, it was a wonder the crystal didn't shatter. Wine splashed in every direction. He glared at her. "I won't have it, do you understand me?"

She gave him a compassionate look. "Maybe you can control your feelings, maybe you can sweep them under the carpet and pretend they don't exist, but you can't do the same with mine. I won't allow that."

His expression turned thunderous. "You won't *allow* it?" he repeated slowly.

Jessie held her ground. "They're my feelings."

"They're crazy."

She shrugged. "Maybe so. In fact, at this precise moment, I'm almost certain you're right about that. I would have to be crazy to fall in love with such a mule-headed male." She gave him a resigned look. "But, then again, there's no accounting for taste when it comes to matters of the heart."

She watched Luke's struggle to get a grip on his temper. In a perverse sort of way, she almost enjoyed it.

"Jessie, be reasonable," he said with forced patience. "It's not me you're in love with. It's the family. I'm taking care of that."

She went perfectly still. "You're taking care of that?" she repeated carefully. "What exactly does that mean? Did you suggest Harlan and Mary adopt me? What?"

A dull red flush climbed up Luke's neck. "No, I...um, I spoke with a private investigator."

Stunned, she just stared at him. Dear heaven, it was worse than she thought. "About?"

He winced at her curt tone. "It was supposed to be a surprise."

"Tell me now." She bit off each word emphatically. She couldn't think when she'd ever been so furious. He'd denied that this had anything to do with his family. So, if she was interpreting all of the stuttered hints and innuendoes correctly, he had decided to get himself off the hook with her by presenting her with her biological parents. Definitely a tidy solution from his point of view. "What exactly is this investigator investigating?"

Luke heaved a sigh. "He's looking for your mother."

At one time that announcement would have thrilled her. She would have leapt from the table and thrown her arms around him for being so thoughtful. Now all she felt was empty. He was expecting her to trade her very real, very deep love for him for a stranger's possible affection. Couldn't he see it wasn't the same at all?

He seemed genuinely puzzled by her lack of response. "I thought this was what you wanted. You said... You told me how much you'd wanted to find your biological family."

"I did. I still do," she said wearily. When she could manage it without weeping, she met his gaze. "But not if it's going to cost me you."

The instant the words were out of her mouth, she ran from the room. Upstairs in her suite, she sent Lara away and took Angela in her arms.

"Can't he see it, angel? Can't he see that the two of you are the only family I need?"

Well, that had certainly gone well, Luke thought in disgust. Maybe he was every bit as bad as Harlan, trying to manipulate lives and control feelings. He'd only wanted to give Jessie the possible—her real family—to make up for the fact that he could never give her the impossible—himself.

After apologizing to Maritza for spoiling the meal she'd worked so hard to prepare, he slowly climbed the stairs. His thoughts were in turmoil... again.

What could he say to Jessie to make her see that it wouldn't work? No matter how badly he wanted her, no matter how much she professed to love him, Erik would always be between them. There would never be a moment when their passion could flower, free from guilt and the overwhelming sense of having betrayed a man they had both loved. If their own consciences didn't destroy them, the disappointment and indignation of the rest of the family surely would.

He paused outside Jessie's suite and listened. He could hear the faint sounds of movement, the murmur of voices. Or was it only one voice? Jessie's, perhaps, as she soothed Angela back to sleep?

Unable to help himself, he quietly opened the door a crack and peered inside. The suite's bedroom was in shadows. A silver trail of moonlight splashed across the bed.

In a corner of the room the whisper of the rocker drew his attention. Jessie was holding the baby to her breast, nursing her. The glow of moonlight made her skin incandescent. Luke's gaze was riveted, his body instantly throbbing with an aching need.

He realized after a moment that the yearning he felt went beyond the physical. He wanted to claim Jessie and the baby as his own with a fierceness that staggered him. He wanted the right to be in that room beside them, to drink in the incredible sight of mother and child in an act as old as time. He wanted...so much more than words could possibly express.

He could deny it from now to eternity and it wouldn't change the truth. Somehow Jessie had realized that and made peace with it, while he still struggled. He knew, even if she did not, that love did not always conquer the obstacles in its path. She would come to see him as a sorry prize, if he cost her the love of his family.

Suddenly he sensed her gaze was on him. When she looked up, he could see the sheen of dampness on her cheeks, and a dismay worse than anything he'd felt over betraying Erik cut through him.

"I'm sorry," he said in a ragged whisper.

The rocker slowed. "For?" she asked cautiously.

The simple question stymied him. For making her cry? For loving her? For refusing to go down a path that could only lead to worse heartache?

"For everything," he said at last.

He turned away then, a dull sensation of anguish crushing his chest. Knowing he was closing the door on so much more than just the sight of the two people he loved most in the world, he quietly pulled it shut.

Even then, though, he couldn't move. In the gathering silence, he heard Jessie whisper his name. It was no louder than a sigh of regret, but to his ears it seemed louder than a shout. He resisted the longing to open that door—the only shield between him and a wildly escalating temptation—for a single heartbeat, then two.

"Luke?"

He closed his eyes and tried to shut out the sound of her voice, but the echo of his softly spoken name was already in his head, driving him crazy. A sigh shuddered through him and he knew he was lost. He opened the door, stepped inside, then closed it.

And as he did, he knew with every fiber of his being that nothing in his life would ever be the same.

Chapter Fifteen

Jessie watched with bated breath as Luke closed the door to the suite behind him. Her heart seemed to have stilled and then, as he took the first step toward her, it began to thunder mercilessly in her chest.

Dear heaven, how she loved him. Earlier tonight she'd been sure that she had lost him forever. She had run out of ways to combat his stubbornness, or so she had thought.

Apparently all it had taken was the whispered cry of his name on her lips, a soft command he'd been unable to resist. He crossed the room, reluctance still written all over his hard, masculine face, and sank slowly to the edge of the bed beside the rocker, careful not to allow his knees to brush against hers. Too careful. It told her how deeply his feelings for her ran and how much he feared losing control.

His gaze remained fixed on the baby in her arms. A soft, tender smile tugged at the corners of his lips. If she could have, without disturbing Angela, she would have touched a finger to that normally stern, unforgiving mouth. She would have tried to coax that smile to remain in place.

"Was it so very difficult?" she inquired dryly.

His gaze found hers. "What?"

"Walking into this room."

"Not difficult," he said, the smile coming and going again like a whisper. "Dangerous. When I'm around you, I can't think. My common sense flies out the window. No one has ever had such control over me."

"I don't think feelings are something you can dictate with common sense," she said.

"Maybe not, but actions are." He studied her with a rueful expression. "You have the lure of a siren, Jessie. You and your baby."

"Is that so terrible?"

"I've told you all the reasons it is."

"Reasons, yes, but you've never said what was in your heart."

Luke sighed and looked away. When he eventually settled his gaze on her again, there was an air of acceptance about him that she hadn't seen before. It gave her hope.

"My heart," he began, then shook his head. "I'm not sure I can find the words."

She leveled a look at him, then said quietly, "Then show me."

A soft moan seemed ripped from somewhere deep inside him. "Jessie, don't..."

"It's just the two of us here in the dark, Lucas. You can show me what's in your heart. There's no one to object."

She thought she detected the faint beginnings of another wry smile.

"Not just two of us, Jessie. Angela's right here with us. Hardly a proper audience for all I'd like to do to you, all the ways I'd like to show you how I feel."

Jessie wasn't about to let him seize an easy excuse for maintaining the status quo. Her entire body shook with her desperate yearning for his touch.

"She's ready to be put down for the night," she countered. "I'll take her into the other room. After that, Luke, no more objections. No more excuses."

She tucked the baby into her crib, caressing the soft, sweet-smelling cheek with a delicate touch. Suddenly she was overwhelmed with emotions—love for this precious new life, love for the man who waited in the next room. Her fear of the future was diminishing day by day.

Finally it was her love for Luke that drew her back. She was lured by the promise of warmth, by the deep sense of honor that made Luke the man he was, a man worthy of loving. There would be no passion between them, she thought with deep regret. Not tonight. Physically for her, it was too soon. Perhaps emotionally, as well, though she didn't think so.

But there would be commitment at last. She could sense it with everything in her. He would no longer deny his feelings. And with Luke by her side, they could fight the rest of the inevitable battle with his family together.

He stood when she entered, then met her halfway across the room. Fighting, then visibly losing one last battle with himself, he opened his arms to her. Jessie moved into the embrace with the sense that she was finally, at long last, home to stay. The serenity that swept through her was overwhelming.

"It won't be easy," he said, his chin resting atop her head as she nestled against his chest.

"Easy is for cowards," she said bravely.

"Anything this difficult may be for fools," he said dryly.

She stepped back and looked up at him. "Do you love me?"

He cupped her face in his hands, then slowly, so very slowly lowered his head until his mouth covered hers. The answer was in his kiss, a consuming, breath-stealing kiss that seemed to last forever and said *yes, yes, yes* with each passing second. The touch of his lips branded her, the invasion of his tongue claimed her as intimately as she knew his body would some day. Relief and so much more washed through her, filling her with wild exhilaration.

Convinced at last, she dared to insist on an answer to her earlier question. "Do you love me?"

"I thought I'd just told you," he said, a satisfied smile on his face.

"That was just a clue," she said, deliberately dismissing the kiss to taunt him. "A very good clue, but not conclusive. I want proof, Lucas."

His eyebrows rose fractionally. "Oh, really? How far can I actually go under the circumstances."

"I'll let you know when you've reached the limit."

"That's what I'm afraid of, we'll reach yours and test mine beyond endurance."

She stripped him of his shirt with slow deliberation. When his torso was bare, she caressed the hard muscles of his arms in a deliberately provocative gesture, following the shape, learning the texture of his skin. "I'd say you're strong enough to take it."

His gaze narrowed. "Do you have a wanton streak I ought to know about?"

"I suppose that's one of the things you'll learn eventually," she taunted him, delighting in the flare of heat in his eyes, the unmistakable catch of his breath that hinted of sudden urgency.

He reached for the buttons of her blouse then and easily freed them. Beneath the cotton, her breasts were fuller than ever and extraordinarily sensitive. He swallowed hard as his tanned, callused finger traced the pale, rounded flesh, arriving in time at the already throbbing nipple. He leaned down and flicked over the sensitive bud with his tongue. A gasp rose in Jessie's throat as she clung to his shoulders.

With her eyes closed and her head thrown back, there was no knowing where his caresses would come next or how shattering they would be. With each exquisite, daring touch, her body responded in ways she'd never expected it to.

Far too soon, she realized the torment she was putting him—putting both of them—through. There would be no tumbling into bed, no tangling of bared arms and legs, no press of bodies on fire. She had un-underestimated how difficult it would be to call a halt. Her newly awakened body throbbed with need. Luke's muscles were tensed with the effort of holding back. His eyes glittered with dangerous emotions.

She covered his hands with her own and stilled his touch.

"Enough?" he asked, his voice hoarse.

"Not nearly enough," she replied, still wondering at the discovery that there could be so much more than she had ever experienced with Erik. "But we're dangerously close to the point when I'll lose all reason."

"How long will it be before I can hold you through the night?" he asked, his voice filled with hunger and perhaps just a touch of awe that such a day would, indeed, finally come. They'd reached a turning point and moved on. There would be no going back from this night. They both recognized that.

"There's been no one in my life, Luke. Not since Erik. I saw no need to ask the doctor about this," she confessed with regret. "A few weeks, I believe."

Luke's expression turned grim. "Just about long enough to put out the wildfire we're about to touch off when everyone figures out what's going on."

Jessie's confidence faltered for a moment. He still hadn't said the words she'd demanded of him. Every action, every touch told her he loved her, but she wanted him to say the words, wanted to hold the sound of them in her heart. "Luke, exactly what is going on?"

He glanced from her bared breasts to her face and back again. "I'd say that's plain enough."

"Just sex?"

"Darlin', there's no such thing as *just sex,* where you and I are concerned. I knew the instant I laid eyes on you years ago that it would be like this between us."

"You know what I mean," she said impatiently.

He pulled her back against him, close enough she could feel his warmth, could feel the steady, reassuring beat of his heart.

"We'll work all of that out," he promised. "One step at a time, Jessie, we'll find our way."

He still couldn't seem to bring himself to say the words. But for now, it was close enough. It was a vow that whatever lay ahead, they would face it together.

Harlan was still at the breakfast table when Luke arrived downstairs in the morning. He knew the instant he looked into his father's eyes that he was upset about something. Luke had a sinking feeling deep in his gut that he knew what that something was. He had thought he heard his parents come in the night before just as he'd slipped from Jessie's room well after midnight. He'd been all but certain he had gotten past them undetected, but perhaps he hadn't been as stealthy as he'd imagined.

His father put the paper aside and waited while Luke poured himself a cup of coffee. Luke deliberately took his time.

When he was finally seated, he met his father's gaze. "Everything okay?"

"I was about to ask you the same question."

"Oh?"

"I saw you leaving Jessie's room last night. I wondered if there was something wrong with her or the baby."

The question might have been innocuous enough, but Luke knew his father better than that. Harlan never inquired casually about anything. And their earlier conversation had already demonstrated Harlan's suspicions. Luke could have manufactured a discreet answer, but he had a hunch his father had already figured out the implications of catching him in that upstairs hallway.

"They're fine," he said, focusing his attention on buttering his toast.

"Then there must have been some other reason for you to be sneaking out with half your clothes in your hand."

So, Luke thought dully, there it was, out in the open. Spelled out in his father's words, it sounded sordid, and his love for Jessie was anything but.

"I love her," he declared defiantly, meeting his father's gaze evenly. "And she loves me."

Harlan sighed deeply, but there was little shock in his eyes. Instead, his gaze hinted of sorrow and anger. "I was afraid of this," he said.

"There's nothing to be afraid of. We're just two people who fell in love. You could be happy for us."

"She's your brother's widow, dammit!"

Luke bit back an expletive of his own. "Erik is dead, Dad. Denying our feelings won't bring him back."

The quietly spoken remarks did nothing to soothe Harlan's temper. "How far has it gone?"

"Not far. She just had a baby."

His father scowled at him. "I meant before."

Luke felt a rough, fierce anger clawing at his stomach. How readily his father was willing to condemn him for a sin he hadn't committed. He supposed that was the price he had to pay for declaring his independence. Despite Jessie's analysis last night, he knew that Harlan would never totally trust him because of that.

"There was nothing between us when Erik was alive," he declared quietly. *"Nothing!"*

"Who the hell are you trying to kid, son? I saw the way the two of you looked at each other. I knew in my gut that was what drove you away, what drove both of you away. You were running from feelings you knew weren't right."

He stared hard at Luke. "Whose baby is it?" he demanded. "Erik's or yours?"

For the first time in his life, Luke honestly thought he could have slammed a fist into his father's face and enjoyed it.

"How dare you?" he said, his tone lethal. "Neither Jessie nor I ever did anything to deserve a question like that. It doesn't say a hell of a lot about your opinion of Erik, either. Whether you choose to believe it or not, he and Jessie had a good marriage. She's not the kind of woman to turn her back on her vows. And I would have rotted in hell before I would have done anything, anything at all to take that away from him."

"Instead, you took away his life."

The cold, flatly spoken words slammed into Luke as forcefully as a sledgehammer. Though he had blamed himself too damned many times in the middle of the night for not doing more to save Erik, the doctors had reassured him over and over that his brother had been beyond help. Hearing the accusation leveled by his father, the same man who'd absolved him from guilt only a day or two before, made him sick to his stomach.

He refused to dignify the accusation with a response. Instead, he simply stood and headed for the door. "I'll be gone before Mother gets down." He glanced back only once, long enough to say, "If Jessie so chooses, she and your granddaughter will be going with me. You can put us all out of your head forever."

"Lucas!" his father called after him. "Dammit, son, get back here!"

Luke heard the command, but refused to acknowledge it. He could not, he *would not* submit to more of his father's disgusting accusations. Nor would he allow Jessie to be put through the same ordeal.

He had known this was the reaction they would face. It was one reason he had fought his feelings so relentlessly. It was why he'd struggled against Jessie's feelings as well, but no more. Those feelings were out in the open now and the fallout had begun. That didn't mean he had to linger at White Pines until his parents poisoned the happiness he and Jessie were on the threshold of discovering.

He was still trembling with rage when he slammed the door to Jessie's suite behind him.

Visibly startled by his entrance and by his obviously nasty temper, Jessie motioned him to silence. "I've just gotten the baby back to sleep," she whispered as she led him into the bedroom. "What on earth's wrong?"

"Pack your bags," he ordered at once. His plan to give her an option in the matter had died somewhere between the dining room and the top of the stairs. He intended to claim what was his and protect them from the righteous indignation they would face if they remained here.

"Why?"

"We're going to my ranch."

To her credit Jessie held her ground. "Why?" she repeated, her voice more gentle. Worry shadowed her eyes.

Luke muttered an oath under his breath and began to pace.

"Lucas, sit down before you wear a hole in the carpet. Besides you're making me dizzy trying to follow you."

"I can't sit. I'm too angry."

"It's barely seven o'clock in the morning. What could possibly have set you off this early in the day?"

"I just came from having a little chat with Dad. Apparently he saw me leaving your room last night and jumped to all the worst conclusions."

"Meaning?"

He frowned at her. "He assumes you and I are having an affair."

"Luke, if it weren't for certain circumstances, we would be," she said pointedly.

"He assumes it has been going on for some time." When she showed no evident reaction to that, he added, "He wonders if perhaps Angela is mine."

Jessie's eyes widened. Her mouth gaped with indignation. Patches of color flared in her cheeks. She flew out of the rocker and headed for the door.

Luke stared after her. "Where the devil are you going?"

"To have a few words with your father. I will not allow him to insult Erik's memory, to insult all of us with such a disgusting allegation."

Luke caught her elbow and hauled her back into the room. "It won't help. He's in a rage. He won't listen."

"Oh, he'll hear me," she insisted in a low tone. "Let me go, Luke."

"Not until you calm down." After a moment, she stopped struggling. Her utter stillness was almost worse. "I'm sorry, Jessie. I knew this was the way he would take it. God knows what Mother will have to say when she finds out. She'll probably insist on going into seclusion from the shame of it all. I think the thing to do is get away until they've had a chance to settle down and digest the news. Maybe then we can have a conversation that won't deteriorate into a lot of ugly name calling."

Jessie's chin tilted stubbornly. "I won't leave. Not like this."

"There's no choice. You have no idea what it's going to be like around here in a few hours. I won't let you go through that."

"I'm not leaving," Jessie repeated adamantly. "I thought Angela would bring this family back together. It seemed to me just yesterday that you and your father were putting past differences behind you. I can't allow our feelings to ruin your chances for a reconciliation."

Luke stared at her incredulously. "Jessie, what the hell is going on here? You fought like crazy to get me to acknowledge my feelings for you. Finally, just last night, we agreed to stop fighting how we feel and try to build a future. Now you're willing to put that at risk so my father and I can get along? I don't get it. Where are your priorities?"

"Where they've always been," she said quietly. "With family. Nothing's more important, Luke. Nothing."

He took a step back and studied her as if she were an alien creature. He didn't understand how he had gotten it so wrong. She was still the woman he loved, all right. Her hair was tousled and just begging for him to run his fingers through it. Her cheeks were rosy, her eyes glinting with determination. She was the most incredible mix of soft curves and fierce convictions he'd ever met.

Right now, though, it seemed to him their dilemma came down to a choice between family and him. If he understood her correctly, she was choosing his family.

Raking his fingers through his hair in a gesture of pure frustration, he shook his head. "So that's it, then? After all this, you're choosing them over me."

He had to admit that Jessie looked shocked by his assessment.

"That isn't what I'm saying at all," she protested. "I'm saying we need to stay here and work it out."

"Not me," Luke said stubbornly. "You can make peace with the devil, if that's what you want, but I'll be damned if I'll hang around with people who think so little of you and of me. Frankly, I'd think you'd have more pride, too."

With one last look in her direction, he turned and stalked from the room. Just as he had with his father earlier, he ignored her plea for him to return. As far as he could tell, there was nothing more to be said.

Only after he had his bag packed and was outside did he allow himself to stop for an instant and think about what was happening. When he did, this great empty space seemed to open up inside him.

They had been so close. He had actually begun to believe that dreams could come true. In the end, though, Jessie's love hadn't been as strong as he'd thought.

He threw his bag onto the passenger seat of one of his father's pickups and dug the keys out from under the mat. He'd hire someone to drive it back from his ranch tomorrow. He sure as hell wasn't about to ask Harlan to have the pilot fly him home.

Besides, the long, tedious drive would do him good. He'd have time enough to figure out how he was going to survive not having Jessie and Angela in his life.

He was just about to turn onto the driveway, when a bright red pickup skidded to a halt behind him, blocking his way. Cody leapt from the truck before the engine quieted.

"Luke, what the hell are you doing?" his youngest brother demanded.

"What does it look like? I'm stealing one of Daddy's trucks and going home."

"Without Jessie?" Cody inquired softly.

Luke stilled and stared at his brother. "What do you know about Jessie and me?"

Cody rolled his eyes. "Hell, Luke, anyone who isn't blind could see how the two of you feel about each other. Don't abandon her now."

"You've got it backward. She made the decision to stay."

"You're the one in the truck, about to head down the driveway," Cody contradicted. "That constitutes abandonment in my book. I thought you had more guts."

A dull throbbing was beginning at the base of Luke's skull. "Whatever you have to say, Cody, spit it out. I want to get on the road."

His brother shot him a commiserating look. "I talked to Jessie a little bit ago. She wasn't making a lot of sense, but I got the gist of it. I know what Daddy said. It was a lousy thing to say. There's no getting around that."

"So you can see why all I want to do is get the hell away from here."

"Sure can," Cody agreed.

Luke was startled by the unexpected agreement. He studied Cody suspiciously.

"Of course, Jessie also told me a story. She said you'd remembered how Daddy taught us to be strong, how he made us fight for the things we wanted in life. She told me some cockamamy theory that he deliberately puts roadblocks in our paths just so we have to scramble over them. It's his way of finding out how badly we want something."

Luke closed his eyes. He recalled the exact conversation all too vividly.

"Isn't Jessie worth fighting for?" Cody asked softly. "Seems to me like she is."

His brother's words reached him as nothing else had. Cody was right. He was running away from the most important fight of his life. Luke sighed and cut the pickup's engine.

"When did you grow up and get so damned smart?" he asked as he climbed from the truck and snagged his brother in a hug.

"Not me," Cody denied. "It was Jessie. She gave me all the arguments I'd need."

"She could have tried them on me herself."

Cody grinned. "She said you were too mad at her to listen. She figured since I was neutral, I might have a shot at getting through that thick skull of yours."

"Daddy's never going to approve of me being with Jessie," Luke said. "Mother's going to go ballistic."

"Ought to make life around here downright interesting," Cody said. "Maybe I'll move back to the main house just to watch the fireworks. Jordan will probably want to come home, too."

"Only if you both intend to stand beside me on this," Luke warned.

A crooked grin on his face, Cody held up his hand for a high-five. "That's what brothers are for."

Luke realized that was something he was finally beginning to understand, thanks to Jessie. It killed him to admit it, but it just might be that she was a hell of a lot smarter than he was when it came to matters of family and the heart.

Chapter Sixteen

Her hands clutched tightly together, Jessie stood at the window of her room and watched Luke and Cody's sometimes heated exchange below. When Luke finally shut off the truck's engine and emerged, a sigh of relief washed through her. She had been so afraid that the desperate call she'd made to Cody had been too late. She'd also known he might be her only chance to make Luke see reason.

She knew from her own conversation with Cody on Christmas that he had given her relationship with Luke his blessing. It had been her first hint that not every member of the Adams clan would be opposed to the feelings she and Luke shared.

This morning she had sensed that even more than Cody's ability to stand up to Luke, what was needed was someone who wouldn't be passing judgment on the original cause of the disagreement between father and son.

As she watched Cody and Luke enter the house, she prayed that all of Cody's skills at persuasion wouldn't be wasted the instant Luke ran into his father.

Drawing in a deep breath, she decided that this was not a battle Luke should have to take on alone. It was their fight. Plucking Angela from her crib, Jessie emerged from her suite and started downstairs.

Halfway down she realized Luke was waiting at the bottom of the steps, his gaze fixed on her. Her pulse skittered wildly as she tried to anticipate what he would say to her. Beside him, Cody shot her a wink and an irrepressible grin.

"I think I'll join Daddy for some coffee," Cody said. "I want a front row seat for the next act."

Jessie smiled at him. "Thanks for coming so quickly."

"No problem. Nothing like tangling with big brother here to get my adrenaline jump started in the morning. Can't wait to get to Daddy now. I might even try to persuade him to let me buy that new tractor I've been wanting."

After he'd gone, Luke finally spoke. "I'm sorry," he said. "I shouldn't have run out and left you to deal with Daddy." The apology seemed to have been formed at some cost. He was watching her uneasily.

Jessie reached out and touched his cheek. "You thought I'd chosen them over you, when nothing could be further from the truth. I chose us, Lucas. We can't have a future if we don't settle this with everyone now. It will eat away at us, until we're destroyed. Hiding away on your ranch is no solution, and in your heart, I think you know that.''

His lips curved in what might have been the beginning of a smile. ''You play dirty, though, Jessica. Threw my own words back in my face.''

''No, I didn't.'' She grinned unrepentantly. ''I had Cody do it. If I could have gotten him here fast enough, I would have had Jordan add his two cents.''

He cupped her face in his hands. ''You are worth fighting for, Jessie. Never doubt that. The way I felt when I climbed into that truck, the empty space inside me where my heart had been, I hope to God I never feel that way again.''

''You won't,'' she whispered. ''I promise.''

Angela stirred in her arms just then. Luke glanced at the baby and his expression softened. ''Come here, sweet pea,'' he said and claimed her.

A look of resolve came over his face as he clasped Jessie's hand. ''Shall we go face the enemy on his own turf?''

She halted in her tracks, forcing him to a stop. ''We won't get anywhere, if you keep thinking of your father as the enemy.''

''How else should I be thinking of him? He's standing square between me and the woman I love.''

The declaration made her smile. ''Try thinking of him as a father who's defending the honor of his son who died.''

Luke sighed heavily. ''In too many ways that makes it all the harder, darlin'. It's almost impossible to fight a ghost.''

Jessie said nothing, just squeezed his hand. She thought she knew how to disarm Harlan Adams, though. And when the time came, she would use Erik's own words to do it.

With Angela in his arms and Jessie at his side, Luke felt his strength and courage returning. He felt whole again. That gave him the resolve he needed to walk back into that dining room and face his father.

His lips twisted into a grim smile as he overheard Cody and Harlan arguing over the need for a new tractor. Cody was cheerfully enumerating a list of reasons to counteract every one of Harlan's opposing arguments. Their words died the instant Harlan spotted Luke and Jessie in the doorway.

"Cody, go and take care of that matter we were discussing," his father ordered brusquely.

For an instant, Cody looked confused. "I can buy the tractor?"

His father shrugged. "Might as well let you do it now, before you drive me crazy."

The tiny victory gave Luke hope. He could see once again that sometimes all Harlan really wanted was a good fight. He wanted to be convinced that a decision was right. If his sons couldn't make a strong enough case, they lost. It might have been pure contrariness, but he sensed that it really was his father's way of seeing that they learned to fight for what they believed in. Maybe underneath that tough exterior, his father really did want only what was best for his sons.

Luke made up his mind then and there that his case for claiming Jessie and Angela as his own would be a powerful one.

"Thought you'd taken off," Harlan said, his tone cool.

His avid gaze carefully avoided Luke and settled on his granddaughter. Luke watched him struggling with himself, fighting his obvious desire to stake his claim on the baby he believed Luke had no right to.

Luke kept his voice steady. "I decided running wouldn't solve this problem."

"Did you reach this decision all on your own, or did Jessie's refusal to go force you into it?"

Luke shot a wry look at his father. "Does it really matter? I'm here now." He glanced at Jessie, seated so serenely beside him. "We're here now."

"You two are going to break your mother's heart," his father said bluntly.

"Why?" Luke demanded. "We've done nothing wrong. Neither of us ever betrayed Erik. We never even let on to each other how we felt until a few days ago. I've been fighting it ever since, out of a sense of honor. It made me crazy, thinking of how Erik would feel if he knew. I couldn't even grieve for him the way I should, because I thought I didn't have the right."

He felt Jessie's gaze on him, warming him with her compassion.

"I think there's something both of you should know," she said softly.

Luke started to silence her, but she cut him off. "No," she insisted. "This is my fight, too."

She leveled a look at Harlan. "I'm fighting for a future for me and for Angela. That doesn't mean we're turning our backs on the past. It doesn't mean we care any the less for Erik. Neither of us will ever forget that he's Angela's father. Choosing to be together just means we're moving forward. That's something Erik understood."

Harlan's face turned practically purple with indignation. "How dare you tell me what my son would or would not have understood! Do you think you knew him any better than I did?"

"Yes," Jessie said.

The quiet, single-word response seemed to startle Harlan as a full-fledged argument might not have. Luke was astonished by her quiet serenity, her composure and their effect on his father.

"Okay, go on and say your piece," Harlan grumbled. "Get it over with."

"I was with Erik when he died," she reminded them. "He knew he wasn't going to make it."

Luke saw tears forming in her eyes, watched as they spilled down her cheeks. She seemed oblivious to them. Her entire focus seemed to be on making Harlan hear what she had to say.

"He knew," she said softly. "He knew how Luke and I felt about each other, possibly even more clearly than I'd admitted up to that point."

"Dear God!" Harlan swore. "That's what killed him, right there. Knowing his wife was in love with another man would be enough to cost any man the will to live."

Jessie shook her head. "No, he gave us his blessing. He said he wanted me to be happy."

"You're making that up," Harlan said. "Damned convenient, since he's not here to speak for himself."

If Luke hadn't seen the agony in her eyes, he might not have believed her himself. He could tell, though, that the memory of those final moments with her husband had tormented her for months now, twisting her up with guilt and self-recriminations.

"It's true," she said evenly. "And if you don't believe me, you can call Doc Winchell. He was right by Erik's side at the end. He heard every word."

A stunned silence settled over the room. Harlan was clearly at a loss. Luke was torn between anguish and an incredible sense of relief that his brother had known about his feelings for Jessie and forgiven him for them. It was as if the last roadblock to his complete sense of joy had been removed. He could feel tears sliding down his cheeks. Unashamed, he let them fall as he watched his father. Not until this moment had he realized how desperately he wanted forgiveness from him, not just for his brother's death, but for this, for loving Jessie.

Harlan finally sank back, his shoulders slumped in defeat. "I don't suppose there's anything I can do to stop you from getting on with a life together," he said grudgingly. "You're both adults. You'll do what you want whether I approve or not."

Luke thought he heard an underlying message in his father's words, a cry for reassurance that their love was deep enough to be worth the cost. He nodded.

"That's true, Daddy. We can get married the way we want. No one can stop us. We can raise Angela and any other children we might be blessed with. We can live happily ever after." He looked straight into his father's eyes then. "But it won't be the same if you're not in our lives. We don't need your approval, but we do want your love."

Jessie's hand slid into his. He folded his own around it and held on tight as they waited for his father's decision. He knew giving in wouldn't come easily to him. It never had. But, as Jessie had reminded him time and again, his father was a fair man.

"It'll take a bit of time," Harlan said eventually. "Some getting used to." A tired smile stirred at the corners of his mouth. "I suppose there's something to be said for keeping Jessica and Angela in the family. She could have gone off and married some stranger."

Luke grinned at him. "I knew you'd find a way to put a positive spin on this sooner or later."

Harlan sighed heavily. "I just hope that's argument enough to keep your mother from going straight through the roof."

Luke stood and settled the baby against his shoulder. "Maybe I'll leave that one to you."

"Sit down!" Harlan ordered.

Luke grinned at them despite himself. "Bad idea, huh?"

Jessie patted his hand. "Remember, Luke, it's a family matter."

For better or worse, it looked as if the whole clan was going to be together through thick and thin. He just hoped like hell that Cody and Jordan settled down soon and took some of the pressure off him. He glanced at Jessie.

"Happy? You got what you wanted."

"We got what we needed," she corrected. "I love you, Luke Adams."

"I love you. And I'll find your family for you, if it's the last thing I do."

"No need," she said. "I've found the only family I'll ever need."

"If you two are going to keep this up, I'm going to leave the room and take that grandbaby of mine with me," Harlan warned. "It's not proper for her to be a witness to your carrying on."

Luke was already leaning toward Jessie to claim a kiss. "Goodbye," he murmured, distractedly.

"'Bye," Jessie said just before her lips met his.

Luke was hardly aware of Harlan's exaggerated sigh or of the moment when his father lifted Angela out of his arms. He had something far more important on his mind—the future.

* * * * *

Be on the lookout for the toddler—and her mother—who steal Jordan Adams's jaded heart. Watch for NATURAL BORN DADDY, coming January 1996 from Silhouette Special Edition.

Dear Reader,

What a joy to be celebrating One Thousand Special Edition books!

As millions of you have come to expect, these are stories of love and laughter, passion and deep emotion. They are every bit as rewarding to write as they are to read.

This is my eighteenth book for Special Edition and the beginning of a series of books about a dynasty of Texas ranchers headed by incredibly sexy, funny, sly Harlan Adams, a man who recognizes his sons' talents and needs often before they do. Under the And Baby Makes Three logo, these books again give me an opportunity to explore not only romance, but family love and loyalty, topics that are central to all Special Editions.

A Christmas Blessing has already given you a first glimpse of the Adams brothers and the father, who has been a powerful influence on all their lives. Next time around in *Natural Born Daddy,* you'll meet Jordan, Houston's most eligible bachelor, who is about to find love in the most unlikely place of all…with the woman who's always been right there under his nose. Cody's story follows in *The Cowboy and His Baby.* And you'll see his sons get their revenge on Harlan for all of his matchmaking in *The Rancher and His Unexpected Daughter.*

I hope you'll join Luke, Jordan, Cody, Harlan and the women and children in their lives as we all celebrate the magic of Silhouette Special Editions.

Sherryl Woods

#1003 JUST MARRIED—Debbie Macomber
Celebration 1000!

Retired soldier of fortune Zane Ackerman's hard heart had been waiting for someone to melt it. Lesley Walker fit the bill so perfectly, he asked her to marry him. But when he needed to right one final wrong, would he have to choose between his past and a future of wedded bliss?

#1004 NEW YEAR'S DADDY—Lisa Jackson
Holiday Elopement/Celebration 1000!

Ronni Walsh had no plans to fall in love again, but that didn't mean her four-year-old daughter, Amy, couldn't ask Santa for a new daddy. And although the sexy single dad next door, Travis Keegan, had sworn off romantic entanglements, Amy was sure she'd found the perfect candidate....

#1005 MORGAN'S MARRIAGE—Lindsay McKenna
Morgan's Mercenaries: Love and Danger/Celebration 1000!

After a dramatic rescue, amnesia robbed Morgan Trayhern of any recollection of his loved ones. But Laura Trayhern was determined to help bring her husband's memory back—and hoped they could renew the vows of love they'd once made to each other.

#1006 CODY'S FIANCÉE—Gina Ferris Wilkins
The Family Way/Celebration 1000!

Needing to prove she'd been a good guardian to her little brother, Dana Preston had no choice but to turn to Cody Carson for help. But what started as a marriage of convenience turned into something neither one bargained for—especially when their pretend emotions of love began to feel all too real....

#1007 NATURAL BORN DADDY—Sherryl Woods
And Baby Makes Three/Celebration 1000!

Getting Kelly Flint to say yes to his proposal of marriage was the easy part for Jordan Adams. Winning the reluctant bride's heart would be a lot tougher. But Jordan was determined to show her he was perfect husband material—and a natural-born daddy!

#1008 THE BODYGUARD & MS. JONES—Susan Mallery
Celebration 1000!

Mike Blackburne's life as a bodyguard had put him in exciting, dangerous situations. Single mom Cindy Jones was raising two kids and had never left the suburbs. The only thing they agreed on was that they were totally wrong for each other—and were falling completely and totally in love....

MILLION DOLLAR SWEEPSTAKES (III)

Are your lips
succulent, impetuous,
delicious or racy?

Find out in a very special Valentine's Day
promotion—THAT SPECIAL KISS!

Inside four special Harlequin and Silhouette February
books are details for THAT SPECIAL KISS!
explaining how you can have your lip prints read
by a romance expert.

Look for details in the following series books,
written by four of Harlequin and Silhouette readers'
favorite authors:

Silhouette Intimate Moments #691
Mackenzie's Pleasure by *New York Times*
bestselling author Linda Howard

Harlequin Romance #3395
Because of the Baby by Debbie Macomber

Silhouette Desire #979
Megan's Marriage by Annette Broadrick

Harlequin Presents #1793
The One and Only by Carole Mortimer

Fun, romance, four top-selling authors, plus a **FREE**
gift! This is a very special Valentine's Day you won't
want to miss! Only from Harlequin and Silhouette.

VAL96

Silhouette

SPECIAL EDITION ™®

CELEBRATION 1000

It's our 1000th Special Edition and we're celebrating!

Join us these coming months for some wonderful stories in a special celebration of our 1000th book with some of your favorite authors!

Diana Palmer
Debbie Macomber
Phyllis Halldorson

Nora Roberts
Christine Flynn
Lisa Jackson

Plus miniseries by:

Lindsay McKenna, Marie Ferrarella, Sherryl Woods and Gina Ferris Wilkins.

And many more books by special writers!

And as a special bonus, all Silhouette Special Edition titles published during Celebration 1000! will have **_double_** Pages & Privileges proofs of purchase!

Silhouette Special Edition...heartwarming stories packed with emotion, just for you! You'll fall in love with our next 1000 special stories!

1000BK-R

Nora Roberts

THE PRIDE OF JARED MACKADE
(December 1995)

The MacKade Brothers are back! This month,
Jared MacKade's pride is on the line when he
sets his heart on a woman with a past.

If you liked THE RETURN OF RAFE MACKADE (Silhouette
Intimate Moments #631), you'll love Jared's story. Be on
the lookout for the next book in the series, THE HEART OF
DEVIN MACKADE (Silhouette Intimate Moments #697)
in March 1996—with the last MacKade brother's story,
THE FALL OF SHANE MACKADE, coming in April 1996
from Silhouette Special Edition.

 These sexy, trouble-loving men
will be heading out to you in
alternating books from Silhouette
Intimate Moments and Silhouette Special Edition.

MORGAN'S MERCENARIES: LOVE AND DANGER
by Lindsay McKenna

Four missions—save Morgan Trayhern and each member of his family. Four men—each battling danger. Would rescuing their comrade help them discover the glory of love?

Watch for the next exciting title in this new series from Lindsay McKenna:

MORGAN'S MARRIAGE (SE #1005)

After a dramatic rescue, amnesia now robbed Morgan Trayhern of any recollection of his loved ones. But Laura Trayhern was determined to help bring her husband's memory back—and hoped they could renew the vows of love they'd once made to each other.

Don't miss the emotional conclusion to this series from Lindsay McKenna and Silhouette Special Edition!

Silhouette
SPECIAL EDITION™®
Holiday Elopements

New Year's Resolution: Don't fall in love!

Little Amy Walsh wanted a daddy. And she had
picked out single dad Travis Keegan as the perfect
match for her widowed mom, Veronica—two people
who wanted no part of romance in the
coming year. But that was *before* Amy's relentless
matchmaking efforts....

Don't miss
NEW YEAR'S DADDY
by Lisa Jackson
(SE #1004, January)

It's a HOLIDAY ELOPEMENT—the season of loving
gets an added boost with a wedding. Catch the
holiday spirit and the bouquet! Only from
Silhouette Special Edition!

You're About to Become a

Privileged Woman

Reap the rewards of fabulous free gifts and benefits with proofs-of-purchase from Silhouette and Harlequin books

Pages & Privileges™

It's our way of thanking you for buying our books at your favorite retail stores.

**Harlequin and Silhouette—
the most privileged readers in the world!**

For more information about Harlequin and Silhouette's PAGES & PRIVILEGES program call the Pages & Privileges Benefits Desk: 1-503-794-2499

Silhouette®

SSE-PP80